THE WRATH OF SHADOWS

✢ ✢ ✢

SAGAS of IRTH

Of Swords and Sorrows

The Wrath of Shadows

The Night's Violin

Beyond the Ivory Shore

Upon the Serpent's Tongue

The Twilight Isle

Lady Midnight

The Song of the Sorians

The Iron Knight

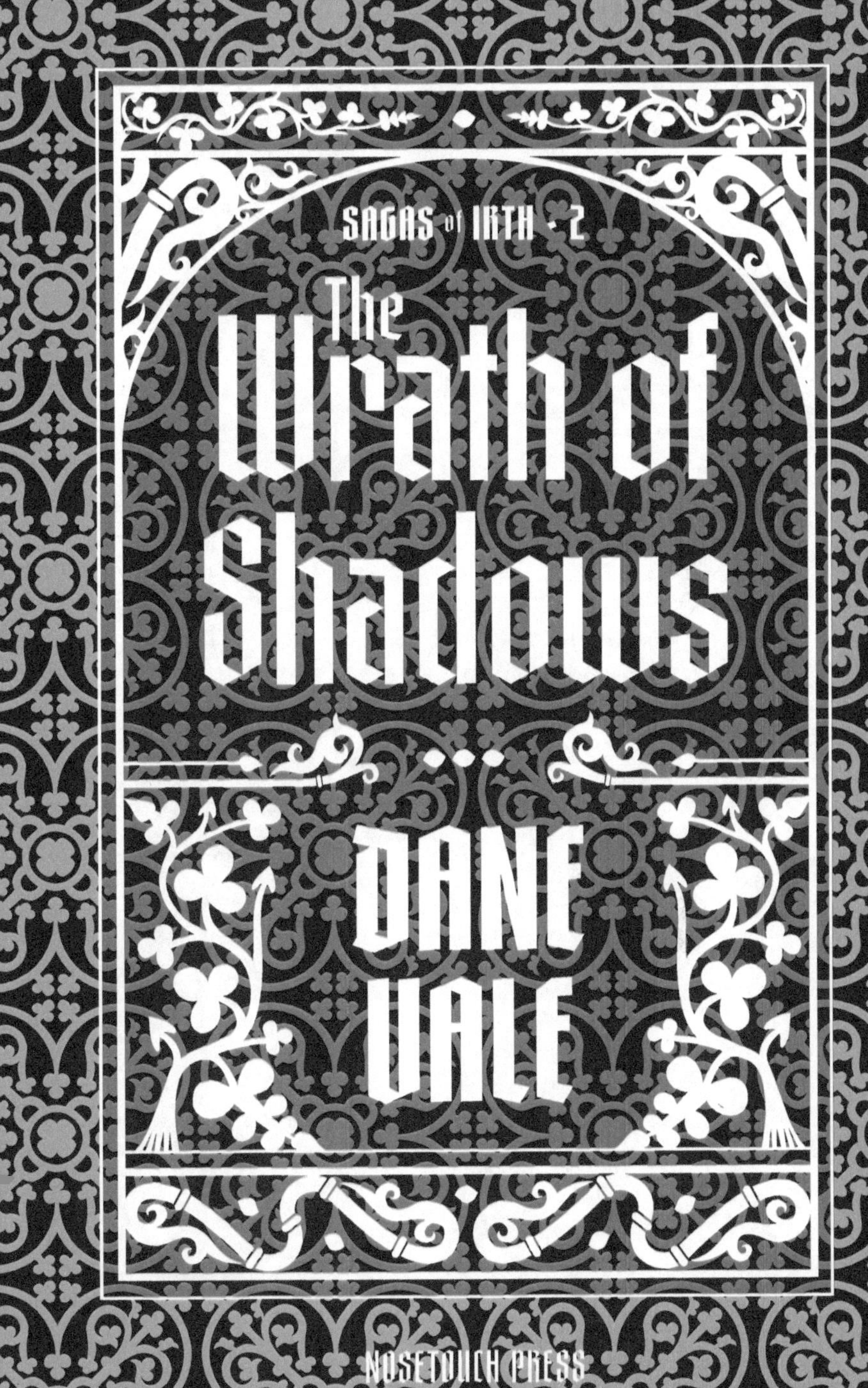

SAGAS of IRTH · 2
The Wrath of Shadows
DANE VALE
NOSETOUCH PRESS
CHICAGO · PITTSBURGH

The Wrath of Shadows

ISBN-13: 978-1-944286-12-5

Published by Nosetouch Press
Chicago, Illinois 60611

www.nosetouchpress.com

For more information, contact Nosetouch Press:
info@nosetouchpress.com

This book is a work of fiction. Names, characters, places,
and incidents either are products of the author's imagination
or are used fictitiously. Any resemblance to actual persons,
living or dead, events, or locales is entirely coincidental.

Cataloging-in-Publication Data
Names: Vale, Dane, author.
Title: The Night's Violin
Description: Chicago, IL : Nosetouch Press [2020]
Identifiers: ISBN: 9781944286125 (paperback)
Subjects: LCSH: Fantasy—Fiction.
GSAFD: Fantasy fiction. | BISAC: FICTION / Fantasy.

Cover, interior, and map design/formatting by Christine M. Scott,
Clever Crow Consulting and Design.
www.clevercrow.com

To Sibyl—
I know you saw it coming!
✛ ✛ ✛

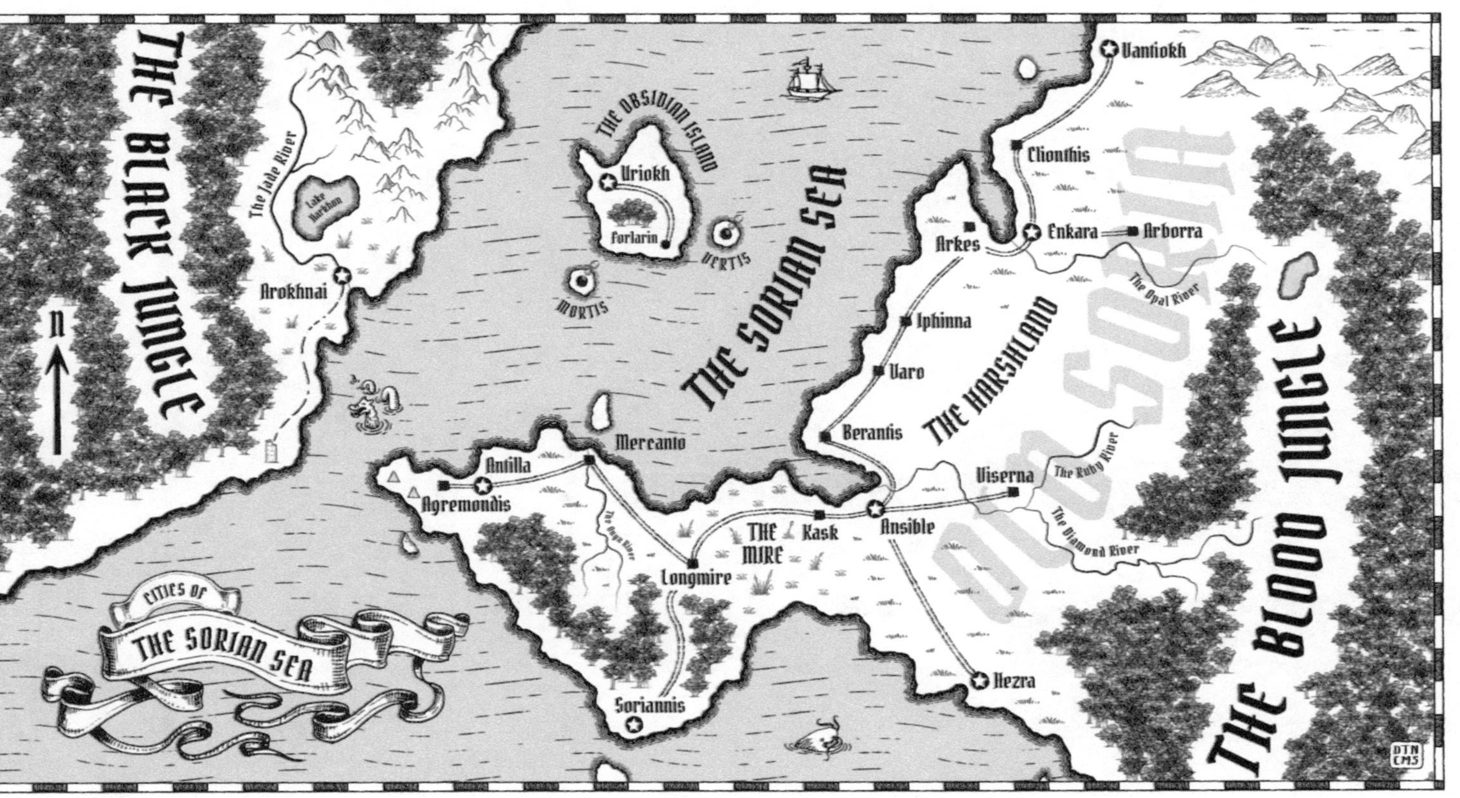

THE BLACK JUNGLE
The Jade River
Lake Marknon
Arokhnai
N
THE OBSIDIAN ISLAND
Uriokh
Forlarin
VERTIS
MORTIS
THE SORIAN SEA
Vantiokh
Clionthis
Enkara
Arborra
Arkes
OLD SORIA
The Opal River
The Ruby River
The Diamond River
Iphinna
Varo
THE HARSHLAND
Berantis
Viserna
Mercanto
Antilla
Agremondis
THE MIRE
Kask
Longmire
Ansible
Hezra
Soriannis
CITIES OF THE SORIAN SEA
THE BLOOD JUNGLE
DTN CMS

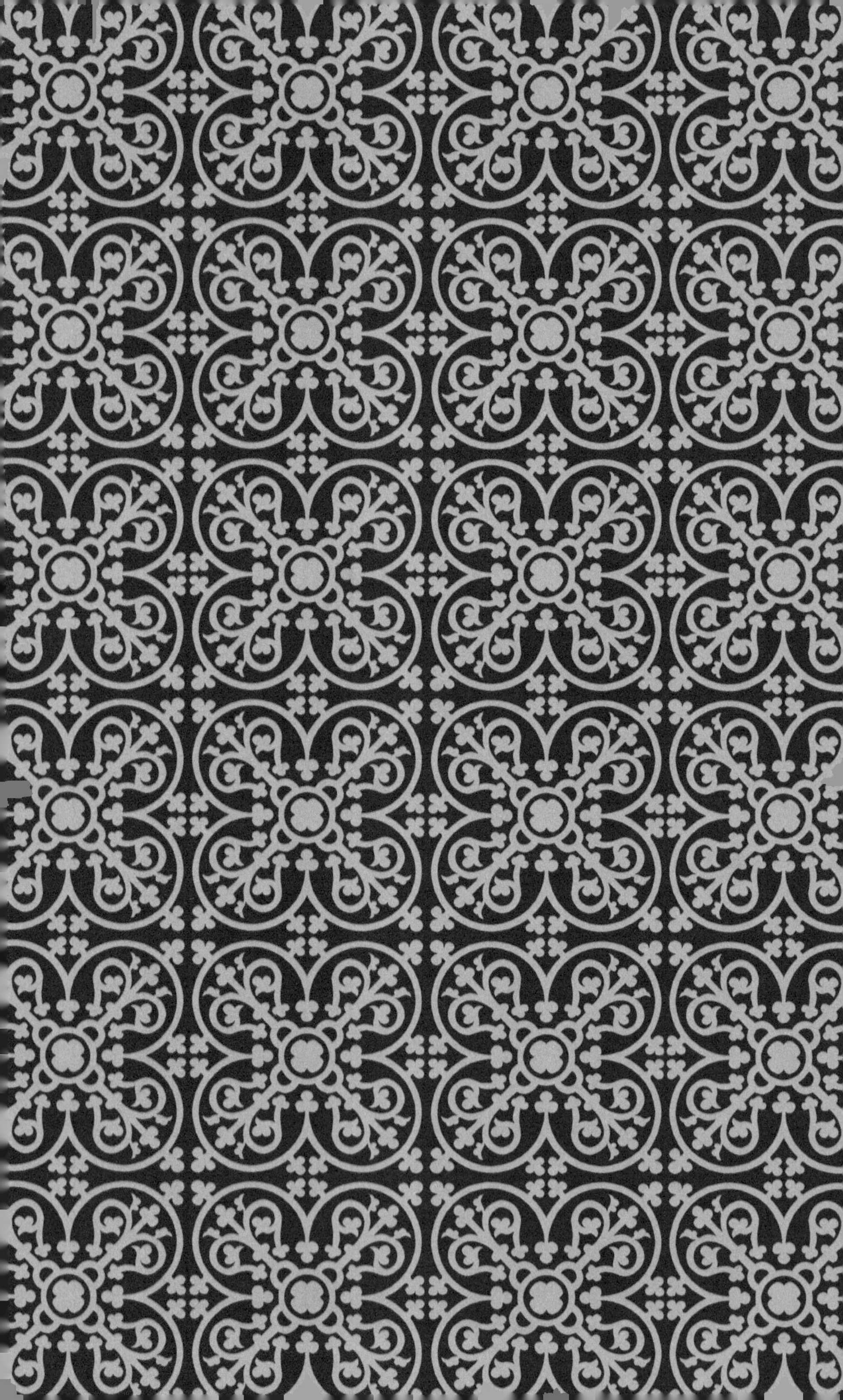

Table of Contents

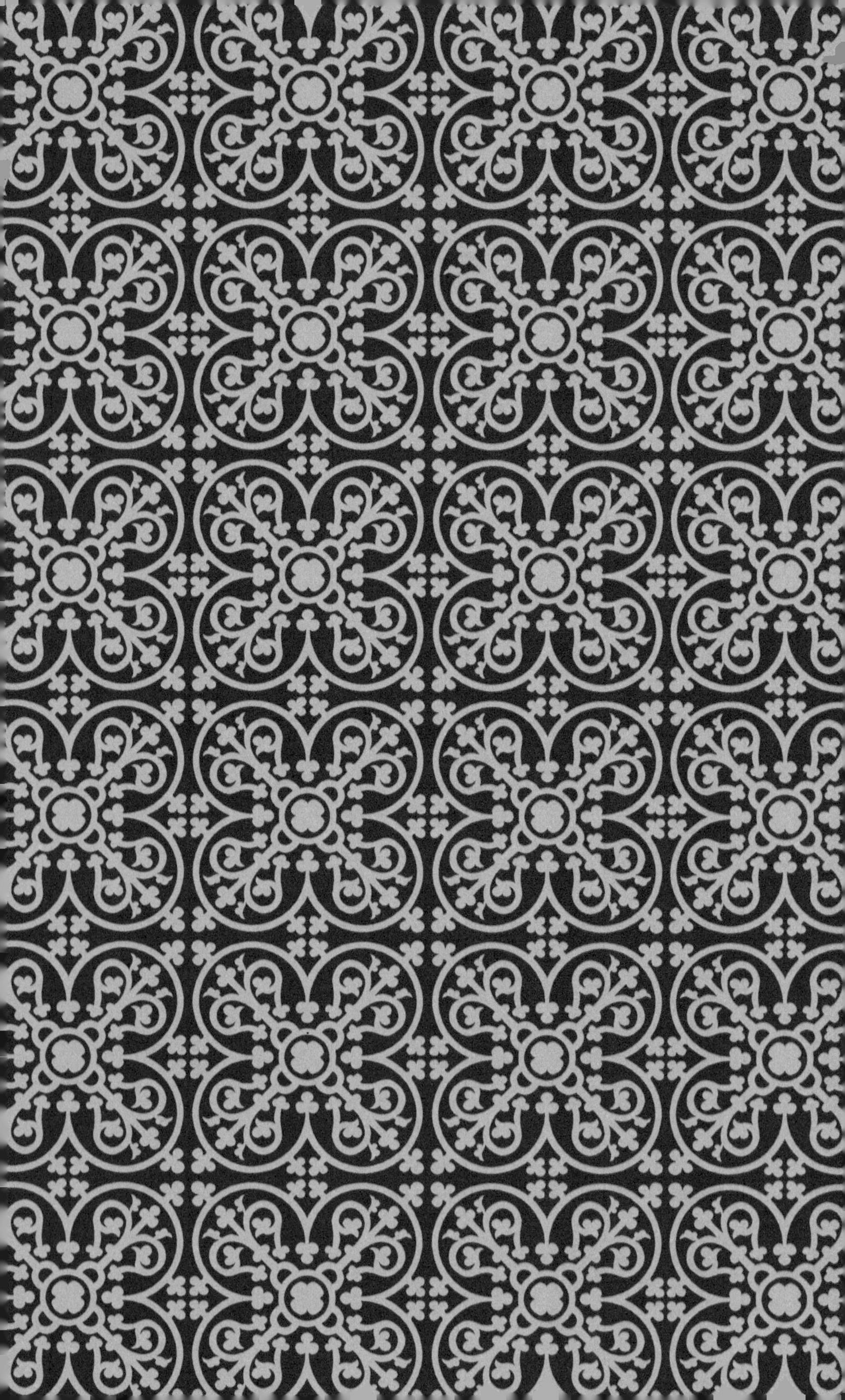

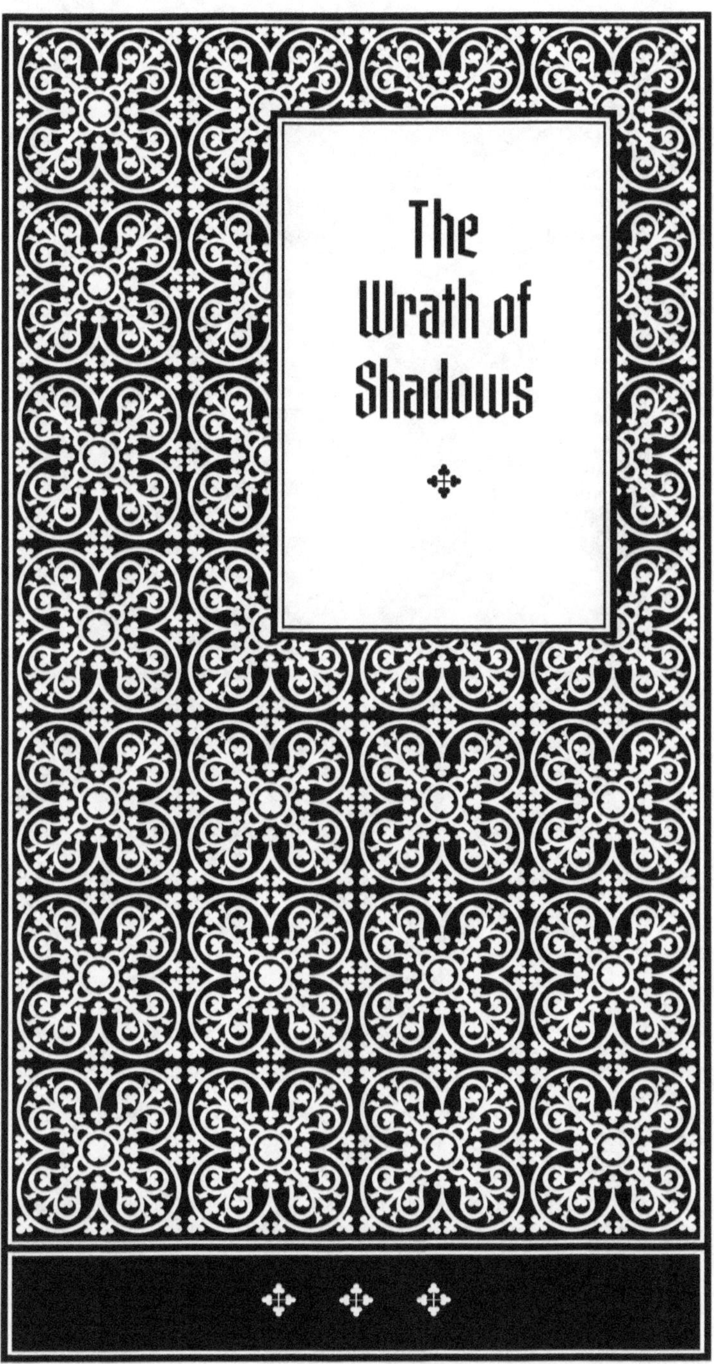

The
Wrath of
Shadows

One

Sometimes, night brought unexpected treasures. Fiss'Q turned her scarlet eyes upon the masked assassin and smiled, the tips of her tiny fangs brushing her lower lip.

Standing in the shadow of the alley behind her home in the city-state of Arokhnai, the assassin—a Smiler—was wearing the signature chalk-white, leering mask of their Southland clan, as well as the black garb that covered them from head to toe. Few were as deadly or renowned as Clan Smile.

The two of them were at a standoff. Fiss'Q stood with her slender, black blade of adamantine drawn and held aloft, and the Smiler with their own curved, silver sword at the ready.

Fiss'Q wore a plum-colored cloak and black leather breeches, her favorite polished black corselet, with purple thigh boots. She stood at least a head-and-a-half taller than the Smiler. Clan Smile's members were invariably small in stature, but it did nothing to lessen their lethality.

"Your play, Smiler," Fiss'Q said. Her dusky complexion and long, ink-black hair let her blend into the shadows even more than the Smiler. Her oval face had an appealing austerity to it, a feral kind of charm that wasn't outright beauty, but was at least a close neighbor to it. Fiss'Q's smile could be as dangerous as her greatsword, and she knew this, and so she smiled at the Smiler, baring her fangs.

It was not supposed to have happened this way, she thought.

The Smiler was supposed to have caught the Shadowlander off-guard, killing her before she knew what was happening. The assassin had lunged at her from the darkness, but she'd seen the attack coming, had been ready for it. Expecting it, even.

Fiss'Q was very hard to catch unawares, and while the Smiler had taken all due precautions to hope to avoid discovery, they had not counted on Fiss'Q's preternatural alertness. This was borne of natural ability and her considerable experience as a Senator in the Republic of Arokhnai, which taught her to be ready for anything, from anyone, at any time.

"You've been marked for death," the Smiler said. By the voice, Fiss'Q could tell that it was a young man who faced her. Male or female, Clan Smile did not play favorites with their choice of assassin.

"You've come all the way from Vantiokh," Fiss'Q said to the diminutive assassin. "You're such a long way from home to die alone on these cobbled streets."

The Smiler lunged at Fiss'Q again, the short blade fire-blackened to avoid reflective glare. It wasn't a bad move. In the narrow alleys of Arokhnai, a quick assassination could occur with nobody the wiser. She would just be one more body for the Deathmen to claim.

Fiss'Q, however, had been ready for the thrust. She brought her slender, two-handed sword down to parry, ri-

posting and forcing the Smiler back before she cut him in half. The narrowness of her sword lent it uncanny speed, as surely as its adamantine alloy lent it great strength.

"Who hired you?" Fiss'Q asked, surging forward, forcing the Smiler to evade the Shadowland warrior.

"We never reveal our contracts and compromise our clients," the Smiler said.

"You've already failed in your mission," Fiss'Q said, pressing her attack upon the assassin. Her black blade whistled as it slashed the air, forcing the Smiler to dodge and parry yet again. "What harm is there in telling me who hired you?"

For the painfully honorable Southlanders, their fate was bound up in the Reckoning Boxes they all carried. They contained a pair of poison vials—one painless, the other painful. Honorable failure earned the painless poison. Disgraceful failure required the painful poison. For Southlanders, suicide was always far preferable to dishonor.

"My dishonor is already apparent in my failure to slay you," the Smiler said. "I wouldn't compound it by betraying my clients, Shadowlander."

A silver-tipped arrow flew at her from another direction, but Fiss'Q had heard the bowstring's muffled twang, and she dodged, the arrow flying at the Smiler, who also evaded it, himself, the arrow burying itself in the plastered brick of the alley.

"Ah," Fiss'Q said, glancing at the Smiler archer perched atop the wall, a black specter drawing another arrow from their quiver. "You brought a friend."

Fiss'Q's mind worked at the prospect of being attacked by multiple Smiler assassins, as she parted the Veil and vanished into the shadows, even as the sword-wielding Smiler lunged at her yet again with a perfect killing blow that nonetheless missed its mark, because she was no longer there to receive it.

The Smiler was too late, circling about in the space Fiss'Q had only just occupied a moment before. Fiss'Q watched from the safety of the Shadowlands, saw the assassins reconvene in the alley. There were not two, but three—a *tralka*. This was a tactical unit for the Southlanders, the minimum necessary to carry out a mission. The third emerged from around the corner, bearing a silver dagger.

That they'd been equipped with silver weapons showed that they at least understood their target, and had prepared. Silver was deadly to any Shadowlander. Not lethal to the touch, but it would harm them. Where ordinary steel proved useless against a Shadowlander, silver could wound them, and worse.

As a Shadowlander, she had access to the Veil, itself the skein between the world that most knew—the here and now—and the Domain of the Shadow Prince. This ability to freely travel between these worlds made the Shadow Masters of Arokhnai a source of fear, wonder, and renown across the Irth.

From beyond the Veil, the world looked just as it always was, but wreathed in shimmering shadow, as if locked in a perpetual twilight. The shapes of the mundane world stood like a lattice of glowing, ghostly architecture. The souls of the people in the everyday world flaring luminously against the all-consuming curtain of shadow that was the Veil.

For a Shadowlander, the living stood out in great, shifting flares of light. Their words could be overheard—as could their thoughts and emotions—as if muffled through gauze. All that they were, wanted to be, wished to be, could be divined by the Shadowlander from beyond the Veil. And the physical world was no obstacle to the Shadowlander, who could pass through objects with ease, as if they were ghosts.

"You've failed, Taltos," one of the Smilers said. "You'd made assurances that you could accomplish the deed without assistance."

Taltos lowered his head. "She's far quicker than I expected."

"She's watching us right now, you know," the bow-wielding Smiler said. "We're all marked for death. You were supposed to kill her with one quick cut, as Trinna instructed, Brother."

The dagger-wielding Smiler, a young woman by her voice, seemed the oldest and most experienced of the three. Why she had not led the attack struck Fiss'Q as curious, and atypical of Smiler protocol. For the ruthlessly professional Smilers, protocol was paramount.

"We should split up, head back in three different directions. Shadowlander she may be, but there is only one of her against our *tralka*."

Fiss'Q watched the Smilers, wondering again who had hired them. She had won many enemies in her time as a Senator in the House of Shadows, and, ordinarily, it would've been an easy bet that the Smiler *tralka* could have done her in. It was easy to get distracted in Arokhnai, where something was always going on.

As a play, it was a worthwhile one undertaken on the part of her enemy—or enemies—but while the Smilers had been careful, they had not been careful enough. This was also not like them. Clan Smile was renowned for the thoroughness of their preparation, and the meticulous nature of their assassinations. Clan Smile's assassinations were almost artful in their conception and execution. This latest effort was a clumsy affair, to eyes as discerning as Fiss'Q's.

"We shall meet at the safe house," Taltos said.

"She knows we're after her," said the Smiler archer. "She will be that much harder to bring down, now."

"Then we should kill her house staff," the dagger-wielding Smiler said. "And thus salvage what we can of this botched assassination. Do you hear me, Shadowlander? Come back this instant, or we will slay your servants."

Fiss'Q's anger flared at that prospect. She was not going to let any harm come to her servants. They were good and loyal to her. These were rare and precious qualities in Arokhnai. She wouldn't stand for it.

Beyond the Veil, the world shimmered and danced, luminous against the sea of black in the shadow in which her kind swam. She rightly assumed the dagger-wielder was the most dangerous of the three, so she attacked her, first.

It was a matter of slipping up through the shadow. She parted the Veil at the Smiler's feet, going at her sword-first. Before the Smiler knew it, she had Fiss'Q's nameless midnight blade passing through her chest, having come up from the ground beneath her feet, from her shadow, itself, seemingly out of nowhere.

And then Fiss'Q was back behind the Veil, while Taltos and the Archer looked on in horror and dismay at the fall of one of their number.

"Trinna!" Taltos said, catching his sister before she fell, as she died in his arms, coughing blood that leaked from the lips of her Smiler mask, bright red against the cold white. The Archer cursed.

"Taltos!" she said. "She's watching us, just as Trinna said. We must flee at once."

"My sister," Taltos said, setting her gently down on the spattered cobblestones. "You shall be avenged."

The Archer took off running, moving quickly and quietly, while Taltos, oblivious in his mourning, leaned over his dead sister, mourning.

Fiss'Q did not feel sorrow at this display. It was not in her to feel compassion for assassins. She understood the nature of their profession more than most, and knew that it was her life or theirs in the balance. If there was no honor among thieves, there was no mercy among assassins.

What remained for her now were the practical requirements of the moment: there were two more assassins, and she would tend to them accordingly. She flitted from the shadows to see Taltos, still hovering over his sister. Only a young Smiler could possibly be so sentimental as to freely grieve in the midst of a mission. Fiss'Q very nearly felt sorry for him.

However, Fiss'Q brought her dark sword down on Taltos, but merely to wound him, cutting his leg, while he was distracted with his dead sister. Taltos let out a cry at the cut, hobbled upon the cobblestones.

Then she dove back into the Veil and pursued the Archer. The Archer, though she was like a shadow among

shadows, trained to within an inch of her life by her clan, she might as well have been drenched in luminous paint, so brightly did her soulfire stand out to Fiss'Q. She was a bright and fearful blur amid the shimmering darkness of the shadowed city.

Fiss'Q caught up with her with the speed and surety of a dark, avenging angel. Passage through the Shadowlands was swifter than in the here and now, which let Shadowlanders cross great distances on Irth with supernatural celerity.

Fiss'Q got ahead of the Archer, and emerged just ahead of her. She came at her with her sword out, to impale her from the shadows. The Archer had made the costly mistake of glancing behind her, as if her pursuer was somehow slower than she was, hot on her heels, and not ahead of her, waiting for her, emerging from the shadows, themselves.

The Archer gasped as Fiss'Q parted the Veil, standing before her, drawing her black sword from the makeshift scabbard of the Smiler's bloody chest.

"Not fair," the Archer hissed, staggering forward.

"Ah, but three-on-one, that's fair," Fiss'Q said. She had no sympathy for this one.

She yanked the Smiler's mask off her face, a most grievous, wounding insult anyone could do to a Southlander. It was a desecration that would give the Archer a nightmare death, knowing that her mask, the very symbol of the Southlander culture, was taken from her while she was still alive. She would be cursed to walk the Irth as a shade, forever denied the mysterious higher honor of her race.

The young woman, white-skinned and white-haired, with pink eyes, was, like all of her people, beautiful to be-

hold, and, coughing blood, her pain and outrage of the insult Fiss'Q had done to her was nakedly apparent in her dying breaths. Few ever saw the faces of Southlanders, although it was not the first time Fiss'Q had gazed upon them. Still, it was the first time she'd ever unmasked a Smiler.

"You're quite lovely, my dear," Fiss'Q said. "Like all of your Southland kin."

The Archer's pink eyes flared with mortally wounded rage, and she snarled at Fiss'Q, blood flowing down her lips, staining her pretty white skin.

"Though we have failed, Death comes for you yet, Shadowlander," the Archer said. "And to your city."

"You first," Fiss'Q said.

"We will be…avenged," the Archer said.

Fiss'Q watched her die, hooking her mask to her belt, letting it sit on her hip while the Archer died in the shadow of the alley.

"What's your name?" Fiss'Q asked. "If you tell me, I might even light a candle in your name in the Hall of the Veiled."

Shadowlanders honored those they killed in the Hall of the Veiled. Their work on the behalf of Arokhnai ensured that there were always plentiful candles burning there, offerings to the ever-watchful Prince of Shadows.

But the Archer was too well-trained to divulge this, and died without another word. Fiss'Q searched her for identifying items, but found only a quiver of poisoned silver arrows, a dagger, a blowpipe loaded with another poisoned silver dart, and her Reckoning Box, a slender, lacquered thing a mere two fingers wide. Fiss'Q pocketed the box and the dagger.

Fiss'Q slipped back within the Veil and flew back to her home, where, incredibly, Taltos was still blubbering by his dead sister, in a pool of his own blood. He had made no attempt to stagger off into the shadows, not that they would have saved him.

Such a lack of discipline from a Southlander was startling. Clan Smile were among the Forsaken—these were the criminal clans of the Southlanders, along with Clans Sigh, Gasp, Smirk, Snarl, and Shriek. The Forsaken had turned their backs on the wisdom of the Preserver, the masked Southland god, and put their highly organized minds to work on crime.

Southlanders had formed the administrative and bureaucratic backbone of the long-lost Sorian Empire, and had survived the extinction of their masters, and the collapse of the Empire, itself. In the millennia since the end of Soria, the Southlanders had insinuated themselves in royal courts and civic councils, offering their organization and expertise. While mainstream Southlanders were content to serve new masters, the Forsaken served only themselves.

Clan Smile was comprised of assassins and bandits. Clan Sigh was packed with courtesans and spies. Clan Gasp was staffed with alchemists and poisoners. Clan Smirk was made up of smugglers and pirates. Clan Snarl was an army of thugs and racketeers. Clan Shriek was full of pitiless mercenaries and torturers. The Forsaken, operating outside the benevolent protection of their god, were always negotiating their carefully contracted services to clients across Irth.

The Forsaken ruled the city of Vantiokh, having been cast out of the other Southland cities by their brethren from the dominant clans. Vantiokh was their bastion, however, at the toe of the Glass Desert and the Broken Lands, the gateway to the North. The Forsaken City was run with ruthless efficiency by those outlaw clans. Under their tightly organized criminality, Vantiokh rivaled even glorious Arokhnai among the city-states of the South.

Fiss'Q emerged from behind the Veil to stand before him, safely out of reach, making sure he saw that she wore the Archer's mask at her hip.

"Torina," Taltos said, gasping. "You killed her as well."

"Of course I did," Fiss'Q said. "I can't let you Smilers go, now can I? You'd never stop until you killed me, my dear. I know how you work."

Fiss'Q moved quickly, slipping Trinna's mask from her dead face, the blasphemous move jolting Taltos out of his grief.

"You dare to insult us in this way?" Taltos asked, while Fiss'Q secured the mask at her hip, a stream of Trinna's blood dripping from its smiling lips as it clattered against Torina's mask.

"Clearly, I do," Fiss'Q said. "Who hired you?"

Taltos pried off his own mask, tossing it at Fiss'Q's feet, landing in his own spilled blood.

"Kill me, end it, now. You think I would betray my clan to the likes of you, Senator?" Taltos asked. "For killing my sister and my cousin, I curse you."

Fiss'Q gazed upon his lovely face, pink eyes welling with still more tears, rivulets traveling down his cheeks. He was so young.

Fiss'Q wondered how the Grandmaster at Vantiokh could possibly have condoned sending these children to attempt to assassinate her. He was fumbling for his Reck-

oning Box when she stopped him with a snap of her hand, prying it away from him.

"Give me that!" Taltos said, but she'd already snatched it away, keeping him at bay with the point of her blade.

"No Reckoning for you," Fiss'Q said. "Not just yet, anyway."

Then it occurred to her—they were freelancing. This attempt had not come from the order of the Grandmaster of Clan Smile or the criminal High Commissioners of Vantiokh. This was the work of three young and ambitious Smilers taking on a contract in hopes of earning repute by dispatching an anointed Senator of the House of Shadows.

"That was your plan, wasn't it, Taltos?" Fiss'Q asked. "Or, rather, dead Trinna's plan. You took a contract on me, in hopes that you younglings would be able to slay me and boost your reputation in Vantiokh."

Taltos paused in his cursing of her to gaze up at her in wonder, and Fiss'Q knew she had the right of it.

"Who hired you?" Fiss'Q asked. "Don't make me ask again, boy."

"You're so smart, Senator," Taltos said. "You figure it out."

He grabbed his dead sister's dagger and made to stab himself in the heart with it, but Fiss'Q knocked the weapon out of his hand with a swipe of the flat of her nameless blade, sending the poisoned dagger tumbling across the alleyway.

"It will be daytime, soon," Fiss'Q said. "Your cousin and your sister will be strung up by their heels in the Courtyard of Consequences. Do you wish to join them?"

"I am already Forsaken," Taltos said. "And I am disgraced in the eyes of the Preserver. I have failed in my mission, have failed my sister and my clan. You think I care what happens to me?"

"In fact, I do," Fiss'Q said, knocking Taltos out with a swat of the flat of her blade.

Two

"Wake up, Taltos," Fiss'Q said, splashing water on the Smiler, awakening him with a start. She had him in her cellar, in a special, secret room behind the wall of one of her well-stocked wine racks. She'd had him cuffed to a chair, arms and legs, using strong manacles. She knew how good Smilers were with knots and ropes. Even manacles might be insufficient to restrain him, if she wasn't very careful.

She had carefully searched him, producing all manner of lockpicks, slender knives, a silver garrote, and a worry stone of fire opal. She had given these to An'Alta, her faithful ward and servant girl, who had secreted them away.

A lone lantern hung from a hook on the whitewashed wall, providing meager illumination.

Fiss'Q gazed at the pale-faced Southlander, who gazed back at her with renewed and wounded outrage and shame. She held his mask in her hands, toying with it, while he squirmed.

"You utterly dishonor me by what you've done," Taltos said. "My sisters and myself, we are cursed for eternity by what you have done."

"I've heard your people consider your spirits to be bound up in your masks. It seems like a risky proposition, given how fragile masks can be," Fiss'Q said. "Just know that I'm keeping this mask. I'm having it mounted with its sisters. It's a rare thing to be able to survive an attack by a *tralka* of Smilers. I'll have to add it to my collection of trophies."

The hateful rage of Taltos Smile coursed through him. It was very much the hallmark of the Forsaken—other Southlanders built careful spiritual cages for themselves in iron discipline, reason, tradition, faith, and ritual. They scorned showing too much emotion. The Forsaken clans, while still possessing the well-ordered minds of their people, marinated in capricious and perilous emotion.

"Who hired you?" Fiss'Q asked. "That's all I need to know."

"I'm not saying," Taltos said. "You'll have to kill me."

"If I wanted to kill you, you'd be dead already," Fiss'Q said. "You can't fault me for defending myself."

She placed his mask on a small table behind her, out of reach, but in his line of sight. Taltos's discomfort was both profound and pervasive.

"We're trained to resist torture," Taltos said. "From an early age, by the very best that Clan Shriek has to offer."

"Of course you are. Such a Southlandish thing to do, to voluntarily torture yourself," Fiss'Q said. "Which brings me to another question. What was your *tralka* doing in Arokhnai, all by yourselves? I've run into Clan Smile before, and I know that it's a rare thing for you to be out and about that way."

Taltos probably thought that giving some semi-useful information would keep Fiss'Q off the scent of her actual employer.

"The Grandmaster deploys us throughout the cities of the Irth," Taltos said. "There are *tralkas* everywhere except Mandria, where the risk of discovery is too great."

"Certainly," Fiss'Q said. "The Dragon is not a welcoming host. So, you were part of a small spy ring operating in Arokhnai."

"Yes," Taltos said. "We monitor Arokhnai for the High Commission in Vantiokh."

Fiss'Q thought about that for a bit, before she replied. Vantiokh was always aggressively engaged in the world around it, and it only made sense for them to deploy Smilers abroad to keep tabs on their rivals.

"However, I should think the most desirable quality of a spy ring would be its invisibility. To remain undiscovered is the most important task for a spy," Fiss'Q said.

"It is," Taltos said. "Trinna found the municipal machinations of Arokhnai to be tedious. She subcontracted out small assignments as they came our way."

"Ah," Fiss'Q said. "Ambition. I like that in a woman."

Taltos glowered at Fiss'Q at her flippant tone, but she was unaffected by it. For all of his considerable training, Taltos Smile was still so green. His inexperience would be his undoing. From her perspective, it already was.

"So, she's the one who made the connections with your client," Fiss'Q said.

"Yes," Taltos said. "I wasn't privy to her negotiations. I was only informed that we'd have the opportunity to assassinate a Senator. Having never done that before, I jumped at the chance."

"Your eagerness was your undoing, my dear," Fiss'Q said. "We of the Shadow Senate are not so easy to kill."

That they had been equipped with silver weapons told her that someone had suitably prepared them for the mission. Silver thwarted their ability to part the Veil, kept them bound to the here and now, in addition to wounding them.

Fiss'Q pulled out Trinna's Reckoning Box, a slender, black lacquered thing which bore her personal seal upon it—a lovely carved flower. Fiss'Q ran her thumb over the carving, savoring the sensation it provided. Seeing it, Taltos squirmed uneasily.

"You should not have that," Taltos said. "It is even more disgraceful than your perverse penchant for mask-taking is your theft of our Reckoning Boxes."

"That's the point I'm trying to make," Fiss'Q said. "You and your kinfolk came at me with poison on your silver weapons. But Shadowlanders are immune to poison. Or didn't you know that?"

Fiss'Q opened the lacquered case, revealing the blue and red vials, lying on a bed of black velvet. Fiss'Q pulled out both bottles, held them up to the light, and unstoppered them. Then she tipped her head and drank them both, while Taltos looked on, aghast.

"Ah," Fiss'Q said. "Piquant, almost refreshing."

She carefully replaced the stoppers on the vials, and put them back in the box, snapping it shut, slamming it on the table, and leaning forward, her ruby red eyes locked on the squirming Smiler, showing him her fangs as she grinned.

"Not smiling now, I see," Fiss'Q said. "You came at me with poison on your silver blades, but had no idea that poison wouldn't hurt me."

"You should be dead," Taltos said. "Those poisons guarantee death to any who drink them."

"I am bound to the service of the Shadow Prince," Fiss'Q said. "When I drank His blood, I consumed a far deadlier poison than anything your people's ardent alchemists might have ever cooked up in their crucibles. Now, how could you possibly have made an attempt upon my life without knowing that you couldn't have hoped to end it with the tools you had? The silver was a good start, but you were unprepared to finish me."

Taltos was brooding over it. "Trinna had been given an elixir to coat our weapons. It was a special thing. She had assured us that if we but cut you with it, you would be dead."

"Who provided this elixir?" Fiss'Q asked.

"The client," Taltos said. "I wasn't there. I only knew what Trinna told me."

There was no poison on Irth that could slay a Shadowlander. Either this was some hitherto unknown poison, or else someone was playing these young Smilers for fools. To equip them with silver weapons had been smart and necessary. However, to provide them with a useless poison was tantamount to cruelty on the part of the client.

Fiss'Q needed to know which it was, but her instincts told her that it was the latter. Whoever the client was, they *knew* that the assassination attempt would likely fail. Fiss'Q, of all of the members of the House of Shadows, was one of the most skilled in combat in Arokhnai.

There were only five members of the Shadow Senate who could possibly be her equal in battle, and none of them were her enemies. Not Q'rr'k, her former master, the Shadow Lord of Arokhnai, nor Hadra Blackspear, nor Vinn Bloodtongue, nor Spartas the Reaver, nor Ky'la Sharp. All of them were on good terms with one another,

and were all faithful protectors of Arokhnai, proven in battle time and again.

"I think you and your kin were being set up as pawns in another's deadly game," Fiss'Q said. "Your client led you astray. You were misled from the outset."

Taltos's face registered his disbelief.

"What are you talking about?" he asked.

"You were set up," Fiss'Q said. "The attack upon me was *intended* to fail. In Arokhnai, it is a capital crime to attempt to assassinate a member of the House of Shadows. The mere act of doing so makes it a matter of state business. The Republic of Arokhnai must respond to it. Somebody wants to engineer a war between Arokhnai and Vantiokh. An assassination attempt might warrant a reaction like that. Now, if you can't—or won't—give up your client, then I must flush them out, myself."

Fiss'Q wondered why she had been targeted. Had the conspirator simply assumed she would have dispatched the assassins, and not taken any alive? Or perhaps it was her close association with Q'rr'k that made her a compelling target.

Did they think that Fiss'Q would go running to the Shadow Lord, demanding revenge? Maybe it was something else—Fiss'Q was well-regarded in the House of Shadows. She could have persuaded Arokhnai to take up a declaration of war against the rival city.

Whoever was behind the botched attempt, they had underestimated her.

Three

True to her word, Fiss'Q had the bodies of Trinna and Torina strung up in the Courtyard of Consequences, for the citizens of Arokhnai to look upon in wonder and derision in the morning. The Courtyard of Consequences was at a nexus of eight streets through Arokhnai. It was a place of summary judgment and reproach, for all to see.

Though the members of the House of Shadows were themselves considered assassins by many, there was a measure of honor embedded deep within their culture. To have hired Smilers to attempt to murder a member of the House of Shadows was an attack upon the Republic, itself.

Fiss'Q intended to make the most of it, as much as she was able, would take it to the House of Shadows, in hopes of flushing out her enemies.

She wore a purple tunic marked with golden wave patterns along its edges, with her golden chain of office around her shoulders, a gold disc inset with polished onyx hanging from the center.

The adornment marked her as a Senator, and Fiss'Q was pleased to see that it retained the power to part a crowd on the busy streets of Arokhnai. She had thought of parting the Veil and appearing at the House of Shadows, but felt a walk down Temple Lane toward the grand dome of the House of Shadows would be more impactful. Let her be seen, so that whoever had plotted against her would know that their plot had failed, and she had survived to see yet another day.

The grand dome of the House of Shadows was made of whitestone, set with blackstone roof tiles that caught the harsh light of the Southland sun. The blackstone absorbed the light of the day and became phosphorescent at night. That green-hued phosphorescence served as a navigational beacon that sailing ships could see at night from afar. It made the seven fabled Towers of Arokhnai look like formidable silhouettes in the darkness of the Sorian Sea.

In the Hall of the Veiled, Fiss'Q indeed lit a pair of candles for Trinna and Torina, to join the dozens that burned that day, to the bemusement of some of the other Shadowlanders, who noted her effort.

"Fiss'Q," asked Jhosia, an older Shadowlander, with long, soot-grey hair bound in a braid, wearing his own purple senatorial tunic and bearing a threefold golden chain from which hung his own disc of onyx. "Were you the one who strung up those Smiler girls in the Courtyard this morning?"

"I was," Fiss'Q said. "You didn't send them after me, did you, Jhosia?"

"Not me," Jhosia said. "But you risk us all by desecrating the Southlanders. Word will get out to Vantiokh about what you did. To have taken their masks is blasphemy, and Clan Smile is not above holding a vendetta, as I'm sure you know."

"Let them come," Fiss'Q said. "I'm more concerned with who hired those Smilers to attempt to assassinate me."

Standing beside Jhosia was Alburelle, a female Shadowlander who was only a few years older than Fiss'Q. Contrasting Jhosia's long hair was Alburelle's own black hair, cropped short. Her red eyes danced across Fiss'Q, her fanged smile revealing nothing beyond her own slight amusement. Alburelle also wore her purple senatorial tunic, much like Fiss'Q's and Jhosia's, but bearing different gold patterns upon them, marking them each as Senators of distinct districts.

"How much is it worth to you to know?" Alburelle asked.

"Do you know?" Fiss'Q asked.

"I could certainly find out," Alburelle said. "You've made so many enemies, young Fiss'Q."

"Not you, I would hope, Alburelle," Fiss'Q said.

Alburelle retained her smile, shaking her head. "I wouldn't dream of crossing Lord Q'rr'k's pet protégé."

"Nor would I," Jhosia said. "Not in a thousand years. I am no warrior, not fit to cross swords with one such as you. You're of Arokhnai's deadliest denizens. You're a veritable jewel in the Shadow Lord's crown."

"Q'rr'k wears no crown," Fiss'Q said.

"A figure of speech," Jhosia said. "You are a national treasure, dearest. On my word, neither fair Alburelle nor I would raise a hand to you."

Smiling, Fiss'Q stared hard at both of them, all the same.

"I'll hold you both to that," Fiss'Q said, while Alburelle and Jhosia smiled back at her. For a moment, the three Senators simply regarded each other in silence, before Jhosia felt compelled to speak.

"What brings you to the House of Shadows, if I may inquire?" Jhosia asked.

"I mean to go to the Shadow Hall and issue a challenge," Fiss'Q said.

"Ooh, a challenge," Alburelle said. "How very primal."

"Decidedly so," Jhosia said. "Positively barbaric."

"You're both more than welcome to attend," Fiss'Q said.

"We certainly will," Jhosia said. "Sadly, the Shadow Senate isn't convening at this hour. You'll barely have an audience at all for your challenge."

"I'm prepared for that," Fiss'Q said. "If you'll both excuse me."

Leaving them, Fiss'Q walked into the Shadow Hall, past the lengthy purple carpet and the polished black-stone columns, past the Chapel of the Shadow Prince, where an idol of their dark god beckoned with a dagger in one hand, and a cup in the other, the hint of a fanged smile on his otherwise stern visage.

She strode past the obsidian statues, to the halberd-wielding Stewards, in their black and silver livery, who respectfully requested that she leave her sword behind. No weapons were permitted within the House of Shadows.

The Shadow Hall was where Fiss'Q's people convened to conduct the political business of Arokhnai. The room itself was round, with the blackest polished basalt forming the floor, in carefully set, interlocking flagstones. Around that were concentric rings of curved, black marble benches, where the Shadowlanders could sit.

Since there were one hundred members of the House of Shadows, the Shadow Hall could seat only one hundred. There were three windows, being primarily purple stained glass, allowing only the barest amount of light in this room. One window depicted Arokhnai itself, in white and golden glass, surrounded by a sea of purple. One window

depicted the Prince of Shadows, in black glass against a field of purple. The third window depicted the sun in gold, the moon in white, and the Irth in black, against a background of purple.

The stained glass windows of the Shadow Hall had stood for a dozen centuries, created by the inheritors of Arokhnai, in commemoration of the fall of Soria. Empowered at last to create their own destiny, the Shadowlanders made the city strong.

Despite the nominal patronage of the Prince of Shadows, Arokhnai had become a republic in defiance of the ruins of the Sorian Empire. This form of government was fiercely protected by the Shadowlanders, themselves. Arokhnai served as inspiration to the Free League city-states of the Northlands, and she had fought many wars and battles to retain her independence from would-be conquerors who yearned to bring back the imperial glory of Soria.

Beyond the benches were candelabras of polished brass, arranged in five alcoves, and topped with fat, white candles. These were tended by the Stewards, who were required to light all of them—of which there were one hundred—when there was a full convocation.

Today, at midday, the Shadow Hall was empty. However, since Fiss'Q had entered, a grey-robed Clerk emerged, as did a Steward, and Jhosia and Alburelle filed in, as well. The Steward waited a moment, then lit three candles.

The great candles threw off a great light in the dark room, and like all light, created shadow. Fiss'Q stood at the center of the basalt circle, and addressed the nearly empty room, once a Steward banged the floor three times with his halberd.

"The House of Shadows convenes at this time," the Steward said. "With three members present: the Honorable Fiss'Q, of the Emerald District, the Honorable Jhosia Longshadow, of the Sapphire District, and the Honorable Alburelle Ar'quesa, of the Diamond District. The Honorable Senator of the Emerald District has the floor."

Another bang of the halberd punctuated the Steward's sentence, and Fiss'Q began to speak.

"Thank you, Steward of the House of Shadows. I, Fiss'Q, Senator of most ancient and prosperous Arokhnai, hereby address those who sent the Southland assassins to attempt my murder in the alley behind my townhouse in the Emerald District.

"Having survived the cowardly and despicable attack, I hereby offer challenge to the aspirant or whomever it was who so conspired to assassinate me. I shall be waiting for them at noontime in the Courtyard of Consequences three days hence, for redress of grievances. Should no one appear at that time, I shall consider the matter settled in my favor, if they are an aspirant covetous of my seat in the House of Shadows.

"If they are challengers conspiring from within this storied hall, I shall take the matter up in a full convocation, and see them pilloried for a most despicable breach of protocol, to have them summarily expelled from the House of Shadows for violation of our most sacred covenants, and exiled from Arokhnai.

"And if it was the work of an outsider, then I declare this attempted assassination to be an unfriendly act to be discussed, debated, and decided in the Shadow Hall, as to how Arokhnai should address this assault upon the body politic."

The Clerk duly noted it, and Jhosia and Alburelle rose to acknowledge it, speaking in turn.

"Our illustrious and most puissant colleague from the Emerald District has been heard," Jhosia said. "Her challenge has been acknowledged and accepted by this august body, to be resolved three days hence, by the tolling of the midday bells of the Great Clock Tower."

"I second the acknowledgment and acceptance of our numinous and eloquent colleague from the Sapphire District and recognize the challenge offered by our illustrious and puissant colleague from the Emerald District," Alburelle said.

Fiss'Q was pleased that they recognized her challenge, and privately wondered if they were the ones who had hired the assassins in the first place. She would take greater pains to learn what she could from Taltos.

"On the matter of the Southland assassins," Jhosia said. "It has been reported that there were only two bodies in the Courtyard of Consequences. However, is it not the practice of Clan Smile to send three assassins? They have a word for it in their convoluted language—a *tralka*. So, what happened to the third member of the *tralka* who so despicably sought to end you in the alley behind your townhouse?"

Fiss'Q had to be careful in this instance, because Jhosia had laid something of a trap for her in that pronouncement. For Fiss'Q to answer honestly could allow for the apprehension of Taltos for official interrogation. This would take him out of her hands and potentially into the hands of those who had hired the *tralka* in the first place. She had no doubt that, were this to occur, the Southlander would die in custody, his secrets unrevealed.

For her to lie about Taltos would mean for her to perjure herself in the House of Shadows, which would itself require a form of redress, which might include censure and her own possible expulsion and exile.

"My numinous and eloquent colleague from the Sapphire District is correct," Fiss'Q said. "The would-be assassin is currently in my custody."

"Ah," Jhosia said. "So, I respectfully put forward that this most invidious assassin be apprehended and taken into the custody of the House of Shadows, that he be properly and thoroughly interrogated, and the matter settled to the satisfaction of all present."

"I second the motion of my most numinous and eloquent colleague from the Sapphire District," Alburelle said. "We shall find out what this person knows."

The clockwork logic of Arokhnai moved forward, which was why Fiss'Q had put forth her lawful challenge three days hence. Regardless of the outcome of the interrogation, she would have her revenge upon those who had plotted against her.

She watched Jhosia and Alburelle, suspecting them of being involved, but not entirely certain. But Jhosia had slipped up, and she had to confront him about it.

"I beg the pardon of my most eloquent colleague from the Sapphire District," Fiss'Q said. "But you referred to the assassin as 'he' a moment ago. How might that have come to pass, given that the gender of the assassin is known only to me? And, of course, whoever hired him."

Jhosia, to his credit, was only slightly embarrassed.

"I apologize to my illustrious peer of the Emerald District," Jhosia said. "I was using 'he' in a neutral context, when I ought to have used 'they' in the spirit of equanimity."

"Still," Fiss'Q said. "My eloquent peer, who seems so knowledgeable in the workings of the Southland *tralka*, might have surmised that the missing member was, in fact, another female. Since he knew that the other two members hanging in the Courtyard were, in fact, female. Logic might dictate that the third member was female."

Jhosia accepted that with a smile.

"My illustrious colleague is, in fact, quite correct," Jhosia said. "Her logic is impeccable, and she is right in assuming that I might have inferred that the third member of the *tralka* was female, and not male. Beyond the aforementioned grammatical tic, I can offer no defense."

"I would put forth a resolution that the would-be assassin remain in my protective custody for three days," Fiss'Q said. "Until such time as my challenge in the Courtyard is answered."

Alburelle gave Jhosia a sidelong look, full of speculative musing.

"I second the motion of my most puissant peer," Alburelle said. "The missing member of the *tralka* shall remain in the protective custody of Fiss'Q for three days, safe from any harm that might befall them."

"This is most irregular, Senator," Jhosia said. "An enemy of the state should be given over to the Grand Inquisitors, at the very least. Given that you were attacked outside of your very home, how can we presume this individual is safe there?"

"I have taken appropriate measures to ensure his protection," Fiss'Q said.

"Still, it is questionable at best," Jhosia said. "The Grand Inquisitors could get to the bottom of the matter in no time."

"For the time being, he's safe where he is," Fiss'Q said. "In fact, I feel that he's safer with me than he might be anywhere else—for I, despite being the injured party, have a vested interest in keeping him alive, that I might know who hired him. Whereas others, particularly his employers, would be heavily inclined to silence him before he might speak and reveal them."

Jhosia was unfazed. A warrior he may not have been, but he was an adroit debater.

"Let the resolution carry," Jhosia said. "Unopposed by any present. However, I would put forth a motion that, while the House of Shadows tolerates this unusual break from protocol, that my illustrious colleague from the Emerald District swears that she will bring no harm to the Southlander, and that he enter into the custody of the Grand Inquisitors of Arokhnai whole and uninjured."

"I second that motion," Alburelle said.

"It is my duty to inform the House of Shadows that the missing member of the *tralka* is already injured," Fiss'Q said. "Having engaged me as he did in combat in the alley. He is wounded at the leg, by my own sword."

Jhosia brightened at that prospect.

"Why, the poor thing must be tended to by a metaphysician or a surgeon," Jhosia said.

"He'll live," Fiss'Q said. "I have tended to his wounds. I merely wanted to inform my esteemed colleagues of his condition, that there might not be question as to his condition upon my relinquishing him from my custody in three days."

Fiss'Q waited, watching Jhosia and Alburelle, trying to gauge their reactions. She was fairly certain that Jhosia Longshadow had, in fact, hired the assassins. Or, at least, was party to it. For Fiss'Q, the challenge at the Courtyard was itself something of a ruse—while she would be there at the appointed time, she really put that out there to try to flush out the conspirators.

"My business here is done," Fiss'Q said. "I look forward to meeting my challengers at the Courtyard of Consequences at noon, three days hence."

Fiss'Q bowed to Jhosia and Alburelle and strode out of the Shadow Hall, recovering her sword as she went. The presiding Steward banged the halberd staff against the floor three times, and his peer snuffed out the candles in the Shadow Hall, one by one.

Four

The masked conspirator entered into the office of the Starslayers, off of Mercenary Row, known as the Garrison District. In this part of Arokhnai, the mercenary companies conducted their business, making contracts with clients and answering constant calls to arms. While ostensibly a peaceful republic, Arokhnai's mercenaries kept busy throughout the year.

There were over a dozen mercenary companies, each sworn to uphold and defend the Republic of Arokhnai, and contractually obligated to provide for the city-state's defense. In addition to the Starslayers, they were the Blackswords, the Sons of Gideon, the Shameless, the Fortunate Ones, the Merciful Sisters, the Swords of Mourning, the Furies, the Dragon's Daughters, the Providers, the Blackshields, the Shadowchasers, and the Gilded Hilts.

All of the companies were in constant competition with each other, and were all regularly reviewed and assessed by the exacting masters of Arokhnai. As a prosperous maritime republic, Arokhnai had a national navy, but the navy itself bristled at the notion of a rival army force, preferring the mercenary system, ensuring a subordinate role for the army.

In the fashion, the mercenary companies vied with each other for contractual favor with the Shadow Hall, instead of turning their energy and attention to wrangling with the navy or with Arokhnai, itself.

The Starslayers were considered one of the top mercenary companies of Arokhnai, having lent valorous service to the republic for over three hundred years. They were as resolute as they were fearless, and campaigned throughout the domains of Old Soria. The black and silver livery of the Starslayers—black helms, silver shields, black tunics, and the symbol of a starburst with a sword run through it, were feared across the region. They were also known for taking whatever contracts were offered to them.

Captain Arven looked over the hooded, masked figure who entered, and assessed them. Arven was himself a young man, clean-shaven in the manner of the Starslayers, and, as yet, unscarred, despite having served for five years in the company. He was handsome and prone to anger, and he was not pleased to see this apparition enter their offices in daylight.

The figure was wearing a burgundy cloak, and wore a Southland mask of unfamiliar origin, bearing a bemused expression on black lacquer. As was the custom of their strange people, no skin was showing, the figure fully wrapped in the robe, and with black gloves and boots. They also wore a golden belt at their waist, from which hung a jeweled dagger in a golden scabbard.

"Can I help you, stranger?" Arven asked.

"I must talk to your Commander Kyree," the figure said.

"And you are?" Arven asked.

"A friend to the company," the stranger said. "I have a contract for you, one that ought to appeal."

"Kyree's away on business," Arven said. "But I'm empowered to treat on behalf of the company in his stead."

"Business," the stranger said. "Of course he would be. There isn't much time. I need your services directly."

Arven glanced at the junior members of the company hovering nearby, their eyes on the stranger as their hands were on the hilts of their swords. Arven rose and waved them off.

"Business, indeed," Arven said. "We welcome business of all sorts, but not to be discussed in our foyer, surely? Let's retreat to the back room, where I might evaluate the contract you offer."

He gestured to the room behind the oaken door on the far wall of their office, and the stranger strode into it with a confidence that gave Arven pause. He commanded his aides to tend to the office in his absence, and followed the stranger into the back room, which was illuminated by a circular atrium window above it.

Arven closed the door behind them, locking it with a key that hung around his neck as a pendant.

The stranger took a seat at the rectangular hearthwood table in the room, upon which were maps of the region, ones penned by Commander Kyree, himself, in his sure-handed fashion.

Arven studied the stranger again, watching the masked figure watch him in turn.

"I do not recognize your clan, stranger," Arven said.

"I represent Clan Smirk," the figure said. "I am Tobias Smirk, of Vantiokh."

Arven searched his memory a moment before replying. Clan Smirk were a pirate clan, smugglers as well.

"You're a long way from Vantiokh, Tobias," Arven said.

"I am, nonetheless, empowered to offer a contract to you," Smirk said. "Three hundred thousand gold sovereigns for the successful execution of said contract."

It was a weighty amount, and Arven felt himself get giddy at the prospect of negotiating such a sum. It would raise his standing within the company. It might even give him the leverage to oust Kyree as the head of the company. Or, at the very least, give him a place among the senior partners, and force Kyree to recognize him as a peer.

"You know our terms," Arven said. "Half up front, half paid upon fulfillment of the contract."

"I do," Smirk said.

"What would you have us do?" Arven asked.

"There is a rival clan member—one Taltos Smile—being held captive in the home of a Senator of Arokhnai."

"And what do you want us to do about him?" Arven asked.

"I want you to abduct him," Smirk said. "And to kill his captors."

The Starslayer captain was empowered to make these decisions on behalf of the company, but the weight of this request felt beyond him. He hesitated.

"Who are his captors?"

The Southlander didn't hesitate in his response, his voice didn't waver.

"Taltos Smile is being held by Senator Fiss'Q, of the Emerald District," Smirk said.

The mercenary nodded, uneasy at the prospect. It was one thing to abduct a person. To assassinate a member of the Senate of Arokhnai? That was another matter. And for that Senator to be Fiss'Q made it even more daunting a prospect. Her reputation as a warrior was known

throughout Arokhnai. Arven would have been challenged to pick a more formidable adversary.

Smirk seemed to sense his hesitation.

"I'm prepared to double the fee of the contract," Smirk said. "Half up front, half upon completion of the task."

Arven looked the Southlander over, who sat impassively, unreadable beyond the smirking black mask that gazed at him. The very motionlessness of the Southlander was unnerving. Arven found Southlanders to be off-putting—one could never trust a people who went around masked all the time.

"Why do you want the Senator dead?" Arven asked.

"That is not for you to know, Mercenary," Smirk said. "Do you want the contract or not? Or do I need to head down the street to the Sons of Gideon?"

The mention of one of their rival companies filled Arven with rancor. He could imagine Kyree's reaction if the Sons of Gideon snared the contract that had been dangled before him.

Still, the city-state of Arokhnai had been good to the Starslayers. Arven may have been a mercenary, but he grew up in Arokhnai, was a native son, and did not relish the prospect of betraying the city. Not even for a sum of gold as great as this. The Senators of Arokhnai were the civic leaders of the Republic, and protected the city, saw that her people and her interests were tended to and protected.

The Southlander sensed his conflict, and applied more pressure.

"Time is of the essence in this contract," Smirk said. "I need it carried out within three days. Ideally, as soon as possible."

In the end, Arven told himself he was a mercenary, first and foremost, and that decided it. He called over one of their clerks, a young man of pale complexion and shorn hair named Sifo.

"Sifo, draw papers for our client," Arven said. "The Starslayers agree to your contract, Southlander. We'll carry out the task at double your fee, half paid in advance."

Five

Fiss'Q returned to her townhouse, where An'alta was waiting, the young girl looking concerned as ever. Her olive skin was sheened with sweat and her braided hair swayed as she shook her head. Her dark eyebrows knitted themselves with her worry, and her fingers worked the horn buttons of her summer tunic.

"Mistress," An'alta said. "The Smiler is getting restless."

"Good," Fiss'Q said. "Let him stew awhile longer. I fear we're going to have a busy few days. Have my armor at the ready. We'll be attacked soon."

"Attacked?" An'alta asked, while Fiss'Q walked over to the shadowbox her servants had made, which held the three Smiler masks, white on a field of yellow, wreathed in blackwood.

"Yes," Fiss'Q said. "By those who hired the Smilers, I should think."

Fiss'Q found a spot on her white walls for the Smiler mask display, where An'alta had already anticipated, having hammered a nail there. How well An'alta knew her!

"You read my mind, An'alta," Fiss'Q said, hanging it up, leveling it. She stepped back, admiring the new additions. "It really looks lovely, doesn't it? Such happy faces the Smilers wear. They are truly the happiest of assassins."

An'alta nodded, glancing uncertainly at the three masks, the middle one bearing the blood on its lips at the insistence of Fiss'Q that it remain.

"It's bad luck to cross Clan Smile, Milady," An'alta said. "This is known throughout Old Soria."

"Very bad luck," Fiss'Q said, smiling at her. "Draw me a bath, and have my armor at the ready, as I instructed."

An'Alta hurried off, while Fiss'Q mulled her options. Were Jhosia and Alburelle conspiring against her? It wasn't unheard of for rivals in Arokhnai to do such things, although it was always considered the height of bad form to do so. Political assassinations within Arokhnai were anathema to its civic culture.

The irony of it wasn't lost on Fiss'Q, knowing full well that she and others had used their talents beyond the Veil to deal with rivals in other regions. But that, to her mind, was different, as it was directed outside the walls of Arokhnai. Within the city was another matter. Arokhnai's Senate allowed for other paths than the cut and thrust of Shadowlandish assassination.

What would Jhosia and Alburelle have to gain by assassinating her? As she saw it, neither of their interests would be served by her death. Jhosia's Sapphire District controlled the textile and dyer guilds, while Alburelle's Diamond District controlled the jeweler guilds. Fiss'Q's own Emerald District was intimately tied to the navy and merchant fleets by its shipbuilding concerns. All three of them controlled rich districts, with more to lose than gain by fighting. Arokhnai was divided up into Districts, which were themselves further subdivided into Quarters.

All of them worked in concert to further Arokhnai's ever-bustling commerce in Old Soria.

Beyond her own close association with the powerful Arokhnai navy, Fiss'Q couldn't see why she might be targeted. Perhaps it was simply that. Control of the Emerald District would give the victor control of the seas around Arokhnai, and of the enterprising merchant fleets that plied their trade around the world.

That had to have been it. The plotters were, through her, attacking Arokhnai herself.

An'alta returned.

"Your bath is ready, Mistress," she said.

Six

Tobias Smirk left the Garrison District with a scroll tube in hand, feeling breathless with the success of his negotiation. The sun was setting, and the shadows were growing long on the streets of Arokhnai.

Already, the members of the Lamplighters Guild were making their way with their brass tapers in hand, to illuminate the streets of the Shadow City.

The Starslayer captain had lived up to his company's reputation, treating with him after all, for the tidy sum of six hundred thousand gold sovereigns.

He wasn't distressed by the money, however. For Clan Smirk, which made its fortune in smuggling and piracy, money was no object. And the money to be made by the disruption of Arokhnai was considerable. It was a pittance, on the balance of things, compared with the opportunities presented to them.

The Southlander went to the harbor, the lovely, protected harbor of Arokhnai, where his ship, the *Arcana*, sat waiting, her black-painted hull lending a predatory cast to the sailing ship.

Smirk felt safer in the Harbor District, in the proximity to the sailing vessels. He felt safest of all on his ship, and came aboard after trotting across the gangplank, where other members of his clan waited, having been put to task preparing the ship for sailing that evening.

His second-in-command, Lucian, greeted him, wearing the white sailing tunics their people wore at sea.

"Captain," Lucian said, saluting. "I trust things went as planned."

"They did," Tobias said. "And we must leave at once, put to sea."

"As you command," Lucian said. The first mate called out orders to the crew, who went about their business with the efficiency that made their people legendary throughout the world. Southland naval crews were among the best at what they did.

"I'm going to my quarters, Lucian," Tobias said. "I'm not to be disturbed. Take the *Arcana* from the harbor and out to sea. Set us on a course north by northeast."

"North by northeast, aye aye, Sir," Lucian said.

Tobias Smirk slipped into his quarters and secured the contract in his captain's chest, putting it under lock and key. He'd paid the Starslayers their half up front with a promissory bank note that Captain Arven had taken with almost shaking hands. Had he not been a Southlander, had they not been in Arokhnai, such a transaction would have been untenable.

No one in the barbaric Northlands would have understood the passing of paper documents as proxies for gold. But that's why Clan Smirk worked in the South, where the remnants of civilization still held on.

It hardly mattered to him that the Starslayers would run to the Bank of Arokhnai and cash that note. They would get their half payment up front, just as he had promised, and they would die in their bid to assassinate the Senator. Of that, he was more than confident.

And that was precisely the point. The Shadowlanders were powerful, but they were not omniscient. They would know that a blow had been struck to their fabled republic, but they would not know from whence it came. It would look like it had come from Vantiokh, and that was all that mattered, as far as Tobias was concerned.

A war between Arokhnai and Vantiokh was just what the region needed. It would provide abundant opportunities for Clan Smirk, who could get approval from the Commissioners of Vantiokh to turn privateer and prey on Arokhnai shipping, and to smuggle contraband into the city-state—it was too perfect, from his perspective. They would create the need by seizing the shipping, and then fulfill the need by smuggling items into the besieged city-state at a premium.

The air seemed to change in his cabin, and a figure emerged from the shadows. Tobias was ready for the intrusion, turned to face it.

In front of him stood a cloaked Shadowlander. For so many, the Shadowlanders filled people with terror. For Captain Smirk, there was only opportunity to be had, and deals to be struck.

"You're early," the figure said.

"I'm punctual," Smirk said.

"The Starslayers are mobilizing," the Shadowlander said.

"As intended," Smirk replied. "They will throw their might against this Senator of yours."

"She's not one of mine," the figure said. "I can assure you of that. Will they bring enough to subdue her?"

"At the price I paid?" Smirk said. "I suppose they might get lucky."

"It doesn't matter," the Shadowlander said. "Should she prevail, I win. Should she lose, I win, as well. It will mean war with Vantiokh, thanks to you."

Smirk had been craving some blackwine, but would not unmask in front of the Shadowlander.

"Do you have my payment?" Smirk asked, holding out his hand.

"Of course," the Shadowlander said, producing another scroll tube. This one was made of bone, and was sealed with a golden blob of wax upon which a Manticore had been stamped, paw upraised, rampant.

Smirk took the scroll and broke the seal, slipping out the document, which he scanned. Southlanders were thorough in their contracts, and the Shadowlander waited patiently while he read it.

"Marvelous," Smirk said. "This will do quite nicely."

"He wants to see you," the Shadowlander said. "Once this business is settled."

"Of course," Smirk said. The Manticore warlord had need of a naval fleet. His armies crisscrossed the Northlands, but the sea was out of the reach of his gilded paws. The Shadowlander had negotiated on Smirk's behalf, giving his clan the sole rights to be the naval fleet of choice for the Manticore, as payment for disrupting the Republic of Arokhnai and throwing Old Soria into chaos. Clan Smirk would soon be swimming in riches.

Tobias rolled the document back up, secreting it into its scroll tube and securing it in his captain's locker.

"We should drink to our good fortune," the Shadowlander said.

"We should, indeed," Smirk said. "But I don't drink with strangers."

"We are all strangers," the Shadowlander said, quoting from the Book of the Preserver. It was practically an insult to do so, when speaking to one of the Forsaken. Smirk let it slide. As the soon-to-be Pirate Prince of Vantiokh, Smirk could afford to be magnanimous.

"What of you, then, Stranger?" Smirk asked.

"I'm back to my city," the figure said. "To watch the festivities as they develop. Should things go as planned, I will tell you who I am in good time, that we may no longer be strangers."

"Then I'll toast your good fortune," Smirk said, reaching for the blackwine, which he poured into a silver goblet. He held the goblet aloft, noting with some satisfaction the discomfort the silver brought the Shadowlander in such close proximity. One bad turn deserved another, after all. Smirk knew silver was anathema to the Shadowlanders.

Smirk lifted his mask and drank deeply of the blackwine, his eyes on the Shadowlander the entire time.

"Until we meet again, Stranger," Smirk said.

"Until we meet again," the Stranger said, parting the Veil and leaving the Forsaken captain alone in his cabin.

Seven

Freshly cleaned, Fiss'Q went to the secret cell to check on Taltos Smile, who had been carefully tended by An'alta and her other servants, under strict instructions to be particularly careful, given the lethality of a member of Clan Smile.

The unmasked Southlander couldn't meet her red gaze with his own pink eyes, instead turned his eyes downward, to her purple knee boots of well-worked leather.

"Your client means to have you killed," Fiss'Q said. "I fear for your safety, should they find you. I'm going to defend my home from them, and, by extension, you."

The Smiler was not placated by this.

"I am doomed," Taltos said. "You should let me partake of my Reckoning Box, and put an end to this dishonorable torment."

Fiss'Q shook her head. "No, Taltos. I will not. I want to know how you came to Arokhnai."

"You won't get that out of me," Taltos said. "My clan has trained me far too well for that, Senator."

Fiss'Q understood that about the Smilers. Even this young one was born and bred to harbor the secrets of their ancient order.

"You are so very young, Taltos," Fiss'Q said. "Are you that eager to suffer for your Clan?"

"I am," he said, smiling at her with youthful defiance. It was all too easy a question to ask a Southlander, even a Forsaken one. In her way, she understood his zeal. She, too, had made her sacrifices, and, seeing young Taltos as her helpless prisoner, she remembered those sacrifices.

"You have no idea what suffering truly is," Fiss'Q said.

In the ruins of Vladikh, farther south than Men ever went, where the oldest Sorian cities had once stood. Vladikh was lodged in the very heart of the Shroudlands, now overgrown with vines and deathwood trees, strangled by the land the Sorians had so effortlessly conquered, long ago. That was where Fiss'Q had been born.

Not born in the sense that they understood it in the North, but it was in ruined Vladikh that she had drunk the Shadow, and had become who she had become, who she always would be, for eternity.

Q'rr'k led them, four of them, through the jungle, moving with an effortless speed that put young Fiss'Q to shame.

"Come, now," Q'rr'k said, protected by the harshness of the day's sunlight by a rust-colored cowl that covered his face. "My darlings can't be tired yet, now can they?"

And, as if to mock them, the skies turned dark and a storm boiled out of nowhere, and a heavy rain began to fall in the dead city, with droplets as big as the fists of men.

Like all of her people, she'd grown up close to the coasts, where it was somewhat safer. Close to the shore, one had only to fear pirates and slavers and the clawed clutches of ravenous fishmen. Coastal cities, where thick, curtained

seawalls offered respite from storm and enemy alike. It was still preferable to going inland, where darker dangers strode through the jungle canopy. A native daughter of Arokhnai, Fiss'Q had only known coastal life, before coming to the attention of Q'rr'k.

The Shroudlands were the darkest remnants of the long-dead heart of Soria, and if Fiss'Q had been inclined to be philosophical back then, which, mercifully, she wasn't—she'd have marveled at how befouled the land was with Sorian magic, even many thousands of years after the old masters had been taken from the world. What had these places been when the Sorians had still walked the Irth, if even the shadowy grandeur of the ruins could be so toxic with rampant magic? Magic dripped from the leaves of trees as readily as water. The soil was sodden with it. Even without the sensitivity of a sorceress, Fiss'Q could feel it.

The four apprentices made their way in the wake of their master, in the driving rain that soaked them all to the bone. Although they were all her rivals, for Fiss'Q, they were also what counted for friends in her world. They were:

Tolon, the oldest, cocksure and confident that he would be the first to drink the darkness and survive among them, with eyes of amethyst and big teeth that pricked his lower lip when he smiled.

Marro, the youngest, and the other girl, with her bleached white hair in four braids, bucking tradition and wearing it long in an act of childish defiance, relying on her nimbleness to evade her adversaries, her smiling sapphire eyes always appraising everything and everyone they met.

And there was Flass'K, who had come from across the river from where Fiss'Q had lived. He had eyes of amber, and had never once complained during their training, had only soldiered on with a resoluteness that Fiss'Q appreciated.

Of course, they had all been lovers, switching back and forth through Q'rr'k's endless training—Tolon with Marro, and Flass'K with Fiss'Q at first, then Tolon with Fiss'Q and Flass'K with Marro, then Marro with Fiss'Q and Tolon with Flass'K, and back and forth a few more times. They sorted things out between them, found and exploited weaknesses and vulnerabilities, formed alliances, broke the same, in a dance that would serve them well for a future in Arokhnai, should they survive the ordeal ahead of them. In Arokhnai, it paid to have the right friends, the right lovers, the right rivals, and, most of all, the right enemies.

Q'rr'k did not care, for it was as much a part of their training as everything else, the understanding that everything flowed, that people could be like wind and water. Everything became something else in time, and best friends could be darkest enemies but for the turn of fickle fortune.

"It is the nature of things," Q'rr'k said, his voice a fervent hiss in the deepening dark that nearly matched his own dark skin. "It will be made plain to you soon enough."

The cyclopean scale of the ruins of Vladikh intimidated young Fiss'Q, although she would not let that fear show in the company of her peers. For aspiring Shadowlanders, any display of weakness would be exploited by friend and foe alike.

The vines were thick as trees, here, and they had to climb them like they were small hills of green and brown

and purple and grey and white—different vines, each redolent of jungle pollen and toxins, and drenched in blood magic. These were things that they would all learn in time, should they survive drinking the darkness.

One was never required to drink the darkness—it was strictly something one could choose to do, if deemed worthy by a Shadowlandish patron. This was understood by all who strove to rise in Arokhnai. For those who did not do it, there were plentiful opportunities to be had—fisherman, sailor, pirate, prostitute, mercenary, assassin, gladiator, scavenger, poisoner, courtier, courtesan, servant—chances to scratch out a living upon the great festering corpse of Old Soria, which sprawled and coiled around them like the long-dead serpent that it was.

But to become one of the powerful elite of Arokhnai, drinking the darkness was the only road to go. The House of Shadows in Arokhnai was only for the elect. Northerners feared and dreaded the Shadowlanders, and with good reason, but they did not understand that in a place as steeped in arcane history as this place was, one needed whatever edge one could hope to get.

Fewer than one in hundreds of souls ever dared to drink the darkness, and with good cause—for most, it meant death. For others, madness. It was a risk, like any other. But the rewards far outweighed the risks. Power. Influence. Immortality.

For Fiss'Q, third daughter in a family of seven children, without wanting to become courtesan-concubines like her older sisters, sold into servitude by their parents for ingots of mercenary gold, drinking the darkness seemed a way out well worth taking.

Q'rr'k had not been an easy master—a mercenary warlord of singular reputation in his company of the Blackswords, he was always in demand, and, thus, had always needed new blood to train, but he had exacting standards. Fiss'Q had welcomed it, and with three older brothers who had been Arokhnai bravos, she liked to think that she knew how to fight.

He had cured her of that conceit early in the training, but had taken a liking to her, just the same, which she had reciprocated, naturally. It was too far a stretch to say that they had been lovers, but they had shared many intimacies in their time together.

"Our way of war is not like that of the Northlanders," Q'rr'k said, while they shared a bed in the city of Ankora, the distant sound of slavers' whips cracking in the lazy afternoon. "They fight with pomposity and passion, make grand games of war. But here, we never lose sight of it, the art and science of strife. And we always play for keeps. Except when we don't. Circumstances make for curious bedfellows, yes?"

Seeing him in that bed, his perfectly dark skin almost purple against the white of the sheets, the scent of blood oranges in the air around them, she'd asked him about drinking the darkness, and he had told her what he knew, which was considerable.

"Come on, Fiss'Q, quit lagging," Marro said, offering to hold out an arm to help Fiss'Q, only to pull it away when Fiss'Q reached for it, laughing, showing her too-white teeth. Marro intended to become a courtesan after she drank the darkness. Foolishly vain, she wanted to preserve her youthful beauty forever by casting her lot in with the Shadow. Fiss'Q had grave doubts about Marro's

ability to draw clients as a Shadowlander, but she had not bothered to share them with Marro, who was determined to have her way.

They reached the temple as the sun had slipped to the horizon, the ground steaming around them, for the rain had moved on, as it always had, and the heat returned, making it hard to breathe in the thick air.

Q'rr'k let them take a last look at the way they had come, pointing the enveloping shadows that grew long as the sun fled the sky.

"Look on your last sunset as mundanes," Q'rr'k said. "Look at how the shadows grow, how they lay claim to everything they touch, until all are drenched in darkness. Such are your lives."

"Lead on, Master Q'rr'k," said Tolon, who had appointed himself leader of their band. In the darkness, Q'rr'k removed his cowl, revealed his features, his garnet eyes and dusky skin that seemed strangely luminescent in the dark. He smiled at each of them in turn, revealing his fangs. All Shadowlanders were fanged, one of the marks of the dark magic of the Shadow Prince.

"You may turn back now," Q'rr'k said. "In truth, to turn away, you need only stay where you are, and wait for me to return. I would *not* recommend heading back through the jungle alone, my darlings. But I say to you, in truth, that there is no shame in staying where you are, and *who* you are. You need not take this step. There are perfect places for you in Arokhnai just as you are. She welcomes all of her children."

"We did not come all of this way for nothing, Master Q'rr'k," Tolon said.

Fiss'Q took the first step into the temple, not wanting to be upstaged by Tolon. Seeing her do this, the others followed suit, while Q'rr'k looked on in amusement.

"My bold apprentices," Q'rr'k said. "Very well. Onward, it is. It is rare that I have so many willing to drink the darkness at one time. Very brave, or very foolish? Who can say? I make no promises on behalf of the Prince of Shadows. Consider that your first lesson on the Path of Shadow."

He held out shiny purple blindfolds for each of them, and told them to take each others' hands, and to follow him.

Compared with their jungle journey, the passage into the heart of the temple was simplicity itself, despite the blindfolds—which were not, in themselves, particularly troubling, for Q'rr'k had taught his protégés how to fight blindfolded.

They traveled within the silent temple, and when the blindfolds were removed, found themselves in a room where an obsidian idol stood, a young man, the Prince of Shadows, who bore a dagger in one hand, and beckoned to them with the other, a fanged leer on his face. He was the patron of Arokhnai, and the city's immortal founder and protector.

In the beckoning hand hung a purple bottle—a crystalline decanter that had a silver collar at the neck and a silver chain that hung from the hand of the Shadow Prince. At his feet, a tarnished silver cup, a goblet of uncertain provenance, etched in unfamiliar runes.

There were lanterns in the room, in alcoves at the periphery, which served only to magnify the shadows in this place. The floor was made of polished black basalt, and Fiss'Q could see her own reflection looking up at her.

No one else appeared to be in the room, but Fiss'Q had the uncomfortable feeling that they were not alone.

Q'rr'k slipped the decanter from the hand of the Shadow Prince, and held it out to them. It was stoppered by a silver cap that was etched in runes that appeared to be like the ones on the goblet, and Fiss'Q could see that within the purple decanter was a liquid of absolute darkness. The liquid seemed to drink the light, itself—far darker than ink or pitch.

"Who will be first to drink the darkness?" Q'rr'k asked.

"I will," Marro said, upstaging all of them with her boldness. Even Q'rr'k was intrigued by her audacity.

"As you wish," Q'rr'k said, drawing forth the silver cup, handing it to Marro. Then he removed the stopper, which hung from its own little chain, and poured a dram of the inky darkness, which flowed like smoke and liquid at the same time. He carefully stoppered it again, while Marro held the cup.

He nodded to her.

"Drink, my darling, knowing that there can be no turning back, once you have drunk the darkness. There are no oaths to take, here, and there is nothing to renounce, for the everlasting darkness claims everything it touches."

Marro's pretty eyes shined as she looked in triumph at all of them. For, however it ended up for them, Marro would always have been remembered as the first to drink the darkness.

She raised the goblet in a mock toast to each of them in turn, and then threw her head back and drank down the darkness, her lips momentarily purpled by it, as she drank her fill.

"It's so sweet," Marro said. "Like nectar."

Fiss'Q remembered that terror, wondering what would happen, wondered if the rumors were true. It was the most secret, most sacred ceremony of Arokhnai. Outlanders would kill to gain the path to the Shadows. Crazed alchemists in the Northlands destroyed themselves trying to replicate the elixir, and yet, her she was, at the dark heart of it all.

Marro handed the cup to Q'rr'k, swayed on her feet, touching her fingers to her temple, her pretty face dimpling as she grimaced.

"What's happening?" Tolon asked.

"She drank deep," Q'rr'k said, his eyes lit with interest, for even he could not guess how it might turn out for his apprentices.

Marro sank to her feet, her skin unchanged, her flesh as it would ever be, for if the darkness had claimed her, they would have known it, Fiss'Q imagined.

"What's wrong?" Marro asked. "What happened? Nothing happened, Master Q'rr'k."

"The Shadow Prince has spurned you," Q'rr'k said. "You are not to be His."

Marro's eyes lit up like fire, and her purple-stained teeth bared in a snarl. "Fraud! Charlatan! Liar! Deceiver!"

She flung herself at him, snapping, gnashing, kicking, and shrieking. Then Fiss'Q saw shadows emerge from some of the alcoves, acolytes who restrained Marro, who was cursing and screaming, hands like claws, manicured nails biting into her palms, drawing blood that dripped on the polished pavestones.

The acolytes dragged her from the room, but her screams could still be heard, echoing in the dark, receding

into unknown places. Marro shrieked and shrieked, and Fiss'Q felt more afraid than ever.

"The Shadow Prince takes a heavy toll on those who would seek Him out this way," Q'rr'k said. "Marro has her life, or what's left of it. Who would risk everything and next take that chalice?"

Tolon stepped forward, refusing to let Fiss'Q get ahead of him again. He gave her a sidelong glance as he did so, the hint of a smirk on his face, while Fiss'Q looked on in wonder. She could still hear Marro's screams, far away, now.

"I will, Master Q'rr'k," Tolon said. "I'm not afraid. Marro was weak."

Q'rr'k smiled to himself, poured another draught of darkness into the cup, into Tolon's waiting hands, while somewhere far beyond them in the temple complex, Marro shrieked like a desolate spirit.

Tolon held aloft the goblet, toasting Flass'K and Fiss'Q in turn, and Q'rr'k.

"I'll see you on the other side," Tolon said, and he drank it down, handed the goblet to Q'rr'k.

All of them exchanged glances in the shadows, Marro's wailing continued from somewhere in the depths of darkness, stilled only by a sound of distant whipping.

"I don't feel anything but cold," Tolon said. "It's so cold."

And then something wondrous happened, as Fiss'Q gasped and pointed at Tolon's feet, which had become as shadowy-black as the polished stone, the darkness creeping up his legs.

"It's working!" Tolon said. "But I can't feel my legs."

It was in that moment that Fiss'Q, glancing at Q'rr'k, understood that something was wrong. Q'rr'k's face registered nothing but a shadowy sorrow.

Tolon tried to step toward them, but where his legs had been, there was only shadow, and he collapsed to the floor with a thump. He was crawling toward Flass'K and Fiss'Q as the shadows crept up his back and over his arms and face, while he managed a mangled scream, reaching a shadow-strangled arm out for them, only to have vanish into a pool of shadow, until there was no trace of Tolon whatsoever.

"I fear that the Shadow Prince has taken our brave Tolon as a sacrifice," Q'rr'k said.

"Where did he go?" Flass'K said.

"He is gone," Q'rr'k said. "Beyond the Veil. He is forever lost. As I have warned you, the Shadow Prince exacts a heavy toll. Are you prepared to pay Him?"

Flass'K looked at Fiss'Q, wiped his hands on his pants. Q'rr'k looked at both of them, a faint smile on his lips.

"Two of you left," Q'rr'k said. "Not so eager, now, are we? Having seen the darkness, will you run from it, embrace the Light?"

"I'm not afraid," Flass'K said. "But I am reluctant."

"Of course you are, my darling," Q'rr'k said.

"Marro was not as weak as some think, and Tolon was not as strong as he believed," Flass'K said. "I can't be sure why the darkness took them in those ways. I must know."

"You cannot know," Q'rr'k said. "None of us can. Even the Sorians could not easily navigate the darkness, and they all but bathed in it. The Shadow Prince has His reasons for what He does, and who He takes with Him to the Shadowlands, and who He rejects. Which of you is next, then?"

Fiss'Q was terrified—the look in Tolon's eyes as the shadow enveloped him would haunt her for the rest of her days. It was a look of panicked desperation, of utter hopelessness, futility, and everlasting despair.

To see his young self consumed by the ravenous shadow was almost more than she could bear. She saw her other life, the one she dreaded and sought to leave behind. Herself as a concubine, serving at the whim of a mercenary lord, raising children who would themselves be pawns in the political parlor games of Arokhnai.

She saw herself growing old and fat and dying, immolated in the way of her people, her ashes returned to the sea. That other Fiss'Q, the one who'd fled from the Shadow, living a normal life, an everyday existence, knowing she'd run from her one chance at immortality. She could not, would not, disappoint Q'rr'k that way, and she banished that other Fiss'Q, the cowardly concubine who had spurned embrace of the Prince of Shadows.

"I'll go," Flass'K said. "I'm stronger than either Tolon or Marro. I'm stronger than Fiss'Q, too."

Q'rr'k accepted this without comment, and poured some more of the inky darkness into the silver cup, held it out to Flass'K, and waited for his apprentice to partake of it.

"I'm not going to give a speech," Flass'K said. "I'm just going to say that where the others have gone, I will not be going."

He upended the goblet and drank, handed the goblet to Fiss'Q in a meaningful gesture, his eyes locked on hers a moment, full of gravitas and the weight of his decision.

Then another look came over his face, and Flass'K's expression changed—it was as if he had been erased. It was as if the darkness had washed over him at once, and laid claim to his mind and his soul.

For one moment Flass'K had been looking at Fiss'Q, and the next moment, he had been looking through her, and then past her, and then, in the end, he had been looking at nothing at all. His legs buckled beneath him and he fell to the ground, gazing across the confines of the chamber, unseeing, motionless but for his breathing.

Fiss'Q cried out, actually dropped the goblet, which bounced on the hard stone with a clang, the lip of the cup dented from where it landed.

"Is he dead?" Fiss'Q asked. "Master?"

Q'rr'k knelt by Flass'K, held out his hand to touch his neck. "He's alive, but I fear that the darkness has claimed him as well, my darling. The Shadow Prince is hungry today."

The master snapped his fingers, and some more dark-robed Shadowlander acolytes came and picked up Flass'K, half-carrying, half-dragging him from the room.

Fiss'Q cried, her tears joining Marro's blood on the otherwise-pristine floor, while Q'rr'k picked up the dented goblet, turned it over in his hands.

"Alas, my hapless apprentices," Q'rr'k said. "And only one left, now. At least you'll have left your mark, when all is said and done. Whatever you fate, you've made a dent not soon forgotten."

He turned the dent around where she could better see it, and smirked at her.

"I'm sorry, Master," Fiss'Q said. She was embarrassed beyond belief at her clumsiness.

"It doesn't matter," Q'rr'k said. "I rather like it. In all the centuries, it amuses me that no one until now has dented the cup. I am glad we could make this bit of history together, my darling. Now, however, it is your turn. There is no shame if you refuse the Prince's gift. The Light

still awaits you, should you turn away from the Shadow. Arokhnai is bathed in both Light and Shadow, as you know—you cannot have one without the other. They are forever bound to one another."

"I want it," Fiss'Q said. "I accept it."

He poured the shadowy elixir into the goblet, and held it out to her.

"Then drink, Fiss'Q," he said, putting the stopper back into the decanter and returning it to the hand of the Shadow Prince with a measure of reverence she had never seen him show before. "There is no turning back from what you have seen today."

Fiss'Q looked at the darkness in the cup, as inky black as in the depths of a cave, and though it appeared to be a liquid, it cast no reflection.

"What is it?" Fiss'Q asked.

"Why, it is the blood of the Shadow Prince Himself," Q'rr'k said. "Isn't it funny that you are the first of my apprentices to even ask?"

Fiss'Q turned the cup this way and that, watching it flow. It was fluid, it was liquid, but it was not water, nor was it wine.

"It is no small thing," Q'rr'k said. "To drink the blood of a god."

"Do gods even bleed?" Fiss'Q asked.

"This one does," Q'rr'k said. "For His chosen people, He does."

"All that bleeds may die," Fiss'Q said. Q'rr'k seemed amused at her comment, smiling both at her, and to himself. He was a philosophical mentor, as much as he was a warrior. It was one of the many things she adored about him.

"Drink now, and you shall never know death," Q'rr'k said.

Fiss'Q would not, could not fear to go where Marro, To-lon, and Flass'K had already traveled. Pride demanded it of her. She would not let them get the better of her, could not return home, chastened, to be married off to a merchant prince or mercenary lord for a bag of gold ingots. That other life was no life at all for her. That Fiss'Q was already dead to her.

She threw back the goblet and drank her fill of it, feeling the intoxicatingly sweet and dreadful cold draught descending down her throat, into her stomach, and spreading out into her heart, laying claim to her soul. In a moment, all sound ceased, and the world around her dropped from view, as if a curtain had fallen. It might have been a moment, could have been an eternity.

And there, standing by her, was Q'rr'k, darkly radiant and handsome.

"My apprentice," Q'rr'k said. "Behold the Veil."

"Did it work?" Fiss'Q asked. "Am I dead?"

"You are beyond death," Q'rr'k said. "You have drunk the darkness, and the Shadow Prince has accepted you as His own. Not as a sacrifice, but as an acolyte."

Q'rr'k pulled them back from the Veil, and they were in the chamber again, in the here and now, and Fiss'Q gazed at her hands, which had taken on a dusky hue, like charcoal diligently dusted with ash.

"I'm alive," Fiss'Q said.

"Not entirely," Q'rr'k said. "But you are most certainly not dead. You are a true Shadowlander, now. Come, and I will teach you how to take your rightful place among the elect in Arokhnai."

He held out a hand, and she took it, and though there was no warmth between their touch, and that cold that had descended with the Veil never left Fiss'Q, she felt icy triumph that she had succeeded where the others had failed.

They made their way through the Shadow Temple to a boat. It was a slender, purple-hulled river runner with grey sails, where Flass'K and Marro had been placed—Flass'K sitting on a barrel, gazing silently at the dark jungle beyond, while Marro was shackled to a stock, whip marks across her back, shrieking in endless agony and boundless rage.

"What happens to them?" Fiss'Q asked.

"We will feed Flass'K to the sea," Q'rr'k said. "For his life has ended. Marro will be bound for the pleasure pits of Ankora, for there is life in her, yet, and she'll fetch a fair price, as so often happens to the Shadow-kissed."

"You cannot possibly cast Flass'K out to drown," Fiss'Q said.

But Q'rr'k's face showed that it was exactly his intention. "When the Sleepless Sleep claims a soul, there is some slim chance that they can be brought back from the void. If they cannot be stirred to swim for their lives, then there is no life left in them, after all. However, if the spark of life returns to him, and he swims, he can be redeemed."

The boat slipped smoothly from its moorings, while Fiss'Q walked across the deck, gazing out at the night's sky with new eyes. Crimson eyes, like rubies.

"Fiss'Q," Marro said, having turned her head to see. Her lovely eyes were wild and wide. "You survived."

"Yes," Fiss'Q said. "I did."

"What about the others?" Marro asked. The words came from her with difficulty, as if pulled by a team of horses.

"Tolon's gone, and Flass'K, well, he's not really here, anymore, either," she said.

"But not you," Marro said.

"You've survived, too," Fiss'Q said.

Marro winced. "I hear voices. A chorus of cries. Do you see the captain's daughter? Hanging on that hook nearby?"

Fiss'Q's eyes turned to a cat o' nine tails that hung from a hook on the mainmast.

"Yes," Fiss'Q said.

"Can you do me a great favor?" Marro asked. "Would you be a dear? She's the only one who stills the voices. She's the only one who still listens."

Fiss'Q looked at Marro's already-whipped back, and at the cat o' nine tails, then back again.

"Please," Marro said. "Don't make me beg. Because I will, I promise you."

Fiss'Q turned her back on her friend and walked away, mindful of Marro's voice trailing after her, her tone growing increasingly strident, the farther Fiss'Q went from her.

"Turn your back on me, will you?" Marro said. "It should have been me, Fiss'Q, turning *my* back on *you!*"

One of Q'rr'k's assistants stilled Marro with a few more lashes, until she was quiet again, and what passed for content, now, in her wounded mind and fractured soul. Marro was strong, and it pained Fiss'Q to see her this way. The coldly mocking cruelty of the Shadow Prince was not something she had expected.

Q'rr'k was not apologetic, gazed at Fiss'Q without emotion, whistling for his mates to pick up Flass'K, who was still unresponsive, as they threw him overboard with a splash, the crewmen watching and waiting for some sign. Fiss'Q said a prayer to the Shadow Prince to give Flass'K

the strength to recover, but He did not answer. Only Q'rr'k's voice cut through the darkness, and Flass'K sank into the depths, never to emerge.

"Onward to Arokhnai, my darling. There is so much to do."

"I will spare you further suffering, Taltos," Fiss'Q said. "We shall see if we survive the night. Then we will continue this conversation. Now, hush."

She extinguished the lantern and left the Smiler alone in the dark, while her own thoughts twisted and turned in the shadows of her mind.

Eight

Upstairs, Fiss'Q went to her sword stand, and took up her slender, two-handed blade. She slipped it from its scabbard, and listened for the Clock Tower of Arokhnai to toll. Sunset would be upon them soon. The shadows would lengthen as darkness descended. She would be ready for whatever came, and whoever dared to darken her door.

"Lock the doors," Fiss'Q said, to An'alta. Don't let anyone in. No matter what."

An'alta nodded, her young face the picture of solemnity.

"Who is coming, Milady?" An'alta asked.

"Enemies," Fiss'Q said."

"What should we do?" An'alta asked.

"Hide and survive. Use some of the other secret rooms," Fiss'Q said. "If anyone breaches the doors, let me know where they are, and I'll cut them down."

Fiss'Q closed An'alta and her other servants into the secret rooms, and positioned herself at her rooftop garden, catching the last glimpse of the sun as it dipped beneath the horizon. In truth, her adversaries would be fools to attack her at night. But, perhaps it was better than attempting it in broad daylight, when more eyes of Arokhnai would be upon them.

She sat before her garden on a wooden walkway, resting her great sword across her long legs, and gently parted the Veil, so that she could see the spirit forces around her. Down below, she could see the luminosity of An'alta and the others, and brooding Taltos Smile, secured in their secret rooms.

Then she saw Q'rr'k standing there, having appeared out of nowhere.

"Fiss'Q," Q'rr'k said, looking down at her, arms folded. Her former master and lover looked as he ever did—lean-built and powerful, his hair cut close and coal-black, his garnet eyes bright, his fangs adding an almost mocking sneer to his darkly handsome face. "What have you been up to, my darling? The Senate is incensed about your declaration. You should have contacted me."

"You've been so busy of late," Fiss'Q said. "I didn't want to distract you from your warring and whoring."

Q'rr'k accepted the barb with aplomb. The two of them had long traded jibes. The Shadow Lord shook his head.

"You're in danger, Fiss'Q," he said. "But you know this, already."

"Are you behind it?" Fiss'Q asked. It was a worthwhile question to ask of him, although she did not think he'd answer honestly.

"Please," Q'rr'k said. "You should know me better than that. If I were, my darling, you would've already been dead."

Fiss'Q tried to keep her attention on their surroundings, and to not let Q'rr'k distract her. So far, there weren't columns of enemies closing in on her home.

"Do you know who is behind it?" Fiss'Q asked. Q'rr'k shrugged. "You wouldn't tell me if you did, would you?"

Her former master shook his head. "As you've so often pointed out to me before, you're no longer my charge, and, therefore, are no longer under my protection. Ergo, I cannot help you in this matter in the manner that I have in the past."

"Then why come at all?" Fiss'Q asked. "To gloat?"

"To warn you that your actions tonight could impact all of Arokhnai," Q'rr'k said. "The outcome of it could be considerable. And, I suppose, I wanted to say goodbye, in the event that you did not survive."

Fiss'Q felt her usual angry impatience at Q'rr'k, who was never there when she needed him most. That he would even appear this way, without intending to assist her, made her want to lash out at him. He smiled, those thoughts and feelings of hers flowing off of her, easy for him to see.

"You do understand that I have no intention of lying down and dying," Fiss'Q said.

"Of course," Q'rr' said. "I would expect no less. But the Prince of Shadows does hate when His children fight. I would ask on His behalf that you consider this, when you have your revenge."

"Duly noted," Fiss'Q said. "You spoke to Him, then?"

"I did," Q'rr'k said. "We sailed together on the River of Broken Promises."

"Sounds lovely," Fiss'Q said.

"It was, strangely enough," Q'rr'k said. "He knows all about you. He's been watching you rather closely. From the very start, you've gotten His attention."

Fiss'Q was disarmed by this, unsure whether to be flattered or afraid. To think that the Prince of Shadows

Himself might have been paying attention to her gave Fiss'Q pause.

"Why?" Fiss'Q asked.

"He finds you curious," Q'rr'k said. "I must admit to being both jealous and envious of you, my darling. Long have I walked in Shadow, and I have strived to have audiences with Him, and yet He inquires about you. After all I have done for Him, you can see why this might cause me displeasure. He's rather fond of you, as gods go. But heed this advice, my darling, if you heed nothing else I say: beware the fondness of gods and the wrath of shadows."

Fiss'Q smiled at Q'rr'k, for he rarely spoke with such cryptic candor.

"Poor thing," Fiss'Q said. "Sorry that I have cost you your hard-won tranquility as you pay homage to our dark Master."

Q'rr'k only smirked, stepping away from her. "They are coming, my darling."

And then he was gone, leaving Fiss'Q alone in the Realm of Shadows, with three dozen bright and battle-angry souls converging on her townhouse from the street.

Fiss'Q was on her feet, moving to the edge of the rooftop. She did not want the intruders breaking into her home and despoiling it, so, she stepped out from behind the Veil, and was back in the here and now in Arokhnai.

"Hey," Fiss'Q called to the bravos below, turning their eyes upward, in her direction. "Up here, you fools."

Acting as impetuously as she'd hoped they would, she heard the twang of bows as dozens of silver-tipped arrows flew upward for her.

She quickly parted the Veil and jumped over the roof, diving for them, brandishing her sword, passing through

the ghostly swarm of arrows that were finding their way where she'd been only a moment before. Had the arrows found their mark, she'd have been dead. That awareness thrilled her.

As fast and well-trained as the archers were, Fiss'Q was far faster, landing safely in their midst in the Shadowlands, their souls shining brightly around her. As she had against the Smiler assassins, she let her sword slash through the Veil ahead of her.

For the bravos, the sword lanced up from the shadowed ground around them, cutting through them before disappearing behind the Veil.

Fiss'Q didn't like to routinely fight through the Veil this way, but when going up against such unfavorable odds, it was necessary.

She hurled herself through the Veil and vaulted over the frightened bravos, who were turning around in disorder, startled by the cries of their mortally wounded compatriots, who were falling all around them.

Fiss'Q's sword cut and slashed at them, her adamantine blade clashing with their steel swords and short fighting spears. She fought them in the bobbing, here-and-there style of the Dance of the Parted Veil. It was the style of the ancient *Vladinakhti*, the Shadow Warriors, akin to threading a needle between this world and the Realm of Shadow, with the sword serving as the needle, and the flesh of her enemies serving as the fabric. Q'rr'k had taught her this dance a lifetime ago, on the Field of Blood.

"You must become a seamstress of slaughter," Q'rr'k said, as they bobbed between worlds. "Back and forth, here and there, nowhere and everywhere, stitching your opponents with your blade."

Back and forth, Fiss'Q sprang and sank, killing nearly half of the bravos before they even knew what was happening to them. The remaining ones formed fighting circles with their spears, back-to-back in three knots of six men, calling out to each other in the lilting tongue of the native Arokhnai.

Fiss'Q regarded the men from safely beyond the Veil, her blade bright with the souls of the newly slain, their shades milling around her in wonderment and confusion at their fate. They had not believed one Shadowlander warrior woman could have brought them to this end as readily as she had.

She could see their commander ordering one of the knots of men to move on the door to her townhouse, with the other two phalanxes serving to provide flanking protection. The fear flowed off the men like shimmering heat waves, rising and swirling up, comingling. The scent of their terror was delicious, distracting.

Their back-to-back formation was, on the face of things, not the worst tactic they could have chosen. It minimized their individual shadows, and with their short fighting spears, made them veritable pincushions. However, for one schooled in the Vladinakhti, the root of their formation still pooled more than enough shadow beneath them for Fiss'Q's purposes.

She demonstrated this by bringing her sword up through the Veil in the midst of the phalanx closest to the front door. Her keen blade hacked at their clustered ankles and toes, maiming the men in a sweep of her sword, sending them down in one group that had the flanking phalanxes filled with startled rage and wanton terror.

Fiss'Q brought her sword up again and again at the fallen men, punching holes through their chests, her sword finding their hearts, drinking deeply of their blood. She emerged before the door, above the newly dead, flicked their blood from her blade, which splashed in a streak against the whitewashed, moonlit walls of her townhouse.

The men were wearing the black and silver livery of the Starslayers, a mercenary company of great repute in Arokhnai.

"Come on, then," Fiss'Q said, as the closer phalanx charged, and the others hurled their fighting spears at her in a furious volley.

Fiss'Q parted the Veil again, dropping into the shadows of the ground, as the silver-tipped spears thudded into the blackwood door. The preponderance of silver weapons meant that they could bring harm to her, if the weapons found their mark. The Shadowlander vulnerability to silver, in addition to wounding and possibly killing, had the ability to tether one to this world, and to bar the parting of the Veil. Should one of their silver weapons hit her, she'd be stuck in the here and now, and at their mercy.

All of those silver weapons also made their attack a potentially expensive enterprise, Fiss'Q thought, meaning that their client had paid dearly for this assault upon her. She intended for the price to be dearer, still.

The second phalanx drew their short swords, while the others were charging for the door.

Despite the onrush of Starslayers, Fiss'Q hacked the sword-wielders from the shadows at their feet, marveling at their continued discipline in the face of her attacks. She brought four of them down, leaping from beyond the Veil

to face down the remaining two, while the other phalanx battered down her front door.

She felt even greater anger at the violation of her home, which was a source of pride and sanctuary for her. All Senators of Arokhnai lived well and took great pride in their homes. Unlike Northland feudal lords, remote in their castles, members of the House of Shadows lived closely among their people, to better know them, hear their concerns, and address them.

The door itself was a sturdy, well-made thing, of thick-cut blackwood that had been carefully carved by artisans of Arokhnai. Replacing it would be pricey, she thought with some amusement at herself, assuming, of course, she survived this night at all.

Fiss'Q's greatsword gave her a reach advantage on the Starslayers with their short swords. She slew the remaining two swordsmen with two crescent-shaped cuts.

The last phalanx had cleared her door. They were surging in, with three of their number raising their fighting spears to try to keep her back, while the other three ran through her townhouse, searching for Taltos Smile.

Fiss'Q made short work of the rearguard, coming up behind them and cutting them down.

"Starslayers," Fiss'Q said. "You've invaded my home. I have killed the rest of you. I recommend you surrender, while you still can."

"Where's the Smiler?" one of them, presumably, the commander, said, from somewhere downstairs.

"Who hired you?" Fiss'Q asked, diving back past the Veil and slipping downstairs, where she saw the remaining three Starslayers, moving in practiced formation, knocking on walls with the butts of their spears to try to find the

hidden doors. They were moving quickly, well aware that they didn't have much time, with a Shadowlander on their heels, hunting them.

Fiss'Q tripped up one of the bravos, grabbing him by the foot with her hand, sending him pitching forward. In so doing, she brought up her greatsword to catch the man as he fell, impaling him on her well-bloodied weapon.

The other Starslayer hurled his fighting spear at Fiss'Q, who deflected it with a turn of her blade. The mercenary drew his short sword and charged at the Shadowlander, whose great blade was at something of a disadvantage in the close confines of the cellar.

The man's face was concealed behind his helmet, but his eyes were bright as he clenched his teeth and forced Fiss'Q back.

"Senator," the Starslayer said. "I am Captain Arven of Arokhnai. I wanted you to know this before I killed you."

"Nice to meet you, Captain Arven," Fiss'Q said. "You do know you're committing treason by attacking me, don't you?"

"A contract is a contract," Arven said, jabbing at her. "Our client has paid us, and we mean to honor it. Treason follows only in the wake of failure."

"Honor and assassination are not comfortable bedfellows," Fiss'Q said.

Fiss'Q drew a black stiletto and parried the thrust of the short sword, knocking the Starslayer on jaw with the pommel of her greatsword. Then she cut the soldier with her black blade, driving it through his foot. He yelled out, calling for his commander.

"Commander Kyree," Arven said.

Fiss'Q cut the man's sword arm with her stiletto, disabling him, turning in time to see Commander Kyree hurl

his throwing spear at her, missing and catching Arven in the chest.

Captain Arven let out a mournful, unbelieving gasp as the spear passed through him, ending his life.

The Shadowlander yanked her greatsword free of Arven's lifeless foot, and ran for Kyree, who, alone, now, was forced to divide his attention between finding the Smiler and defending himself from Fiss'Q.

"Who hired you?" Fiss'Q asked. "Tell me this and I'll spare you."

The commander pondered it for a moment. Then, Kyree threw off his helmet, threw down his weapon, both of which clanged on the amberwood floor. His almost-handsome face bore a lateral scar across his cheeks and nose, his blue eyes wild with fear-fueled anger, his hair cut razor-close to his tattooed scalp.

A mercenary to the end, he gave up his employer in a heartbeat.

Nine

The *Arcana* had been sailing north by northeast, as Captain Smirk had commanded. The Captain had been in his quarters, planning the trip back to Vantiokh by the most efficient means. Forsaken he may have been, but Smirk was a most capable and diligent navigator. Without a benevolent Preserver to protect them, the Forsaken had only their minds, their wits, their discipline, and their clans to see them through.

Upon his captain's table was one of his well-used maps, and he studied them by lantern light, noting the speediest possible routes.

There came a knock at his door.

"Come in," Smirk said, hand on the pommel of the dagger he always kept at his hip. Lucian appeared, saluting his captain.

"Begging your pardon, Captain, but we are at the course you gave us," Lucian said.

"Naturally," Smirk said. "Hold us north by northeast, keeping to twenty-five degrees, until we reach Vantiokh."

"As you command, Sir," Lucian said, saluting and closing the door.

Satisfied, Smirk slipped off his mask and rested it on the table, pouring himself some blackwine. Only in the most private of circumstances would the Southlanders ever willingly remove their masks. It was an ancestral tradition that harkened back to their days as the slaves of the Sorians. The masks, a token of their shame as bonded servants of Soria, over time, had become badges of their station. Over the centuries, they had gradually become badges of honor, distinguishing the Southland clans in their chosen vocations. For Clan Smirk, it was even more than that. It was an assurance that one was not to trifle with them in matters of war and profit. The Smirks would always come out ahead in the end. It was how they'd earned their name.

Tobias eyed the smirking mask of his clan, feeling the mockery of the mask as it looked up at him sightlessly. For Clan Smirk, there was always another opportunity for the last laugh. The war he'd planned between Arokhnai and Vantiokh would be no different. He and his kin would, indeed, have much to smirk about soon enough. The profits to be taken in such a war would be mammoth.

It was thirsty work, planning a war, but he was sure that he personally would profit handsomely from it, once the blood dried and the dust settled. For a Forsaken son of distant Vantiokh, it was more than sufficient. The elders of his clan would be happy at what he had achieved on the shores of Arokhnai.

The air in his cabin stirred, however, and Smirk grabbed his mask and slipped it back on his face as the Veil parted, and, once again, the Stranger was standing in his quarters.

"Welcome, Stranger," Smirk said, raising his goblet. "I trust matters were resolved to your satisfaction?"

"They were," the Stranger said. "Your mercenaries failed in their mission."

"They weren't my mercenaries, Stranger," Smirk said. "They were some of Arokhnai's finest, by my estimation."

"She cut them down as expected," the Stranger said. "You are now implicated in the plot. You have been identified by their Commander Kyree."

"Again, as intended," Smirk said, watching the Shadowlander closely. "Are we to be strangers, still, or will you tell me who you are?"

"No," the Stranger said. "I just wanted you to know what had transpired. You are bound for Vantiokh, are you not?"

"You know I am," Smirk said. "I long to leave these green waters for the deeper blues of my native sea."

"They will hunt you," the Stranger said. "You must not betray me."

"How can I betray you?" Smirk asked. "I hardly know you."

"But you know of me," the Stranger said. "And that could be enough."

"Enough for what?" Smirk asked.

The Shadowlander watched him from across the table, and, as yet, made no threatening moves. But Tobias felt threatened by the Shadowlander's presence, all the same. He could see how Shadowlanders could be thought of with such dread and terror in other circles, sharing this space with this one, in what ought to have been the security of his cabin.

"My people have many ways of getting people to talk," the Stranger said.

"As do mine," Smirk said.

"It's perhaps safer for me if you were dead," the Stranger said, drawing a dagger that glistened.

But while Smirk didn't know the poison likely on the dagger, he was entirely familiar with poisoned daggers, and the propensity of those inclined to use them.

"Please," Smirk said, with mockery in his voice. "You hope to threaten one of the Forsaken with poison and assassination? We grow up with it, Stranger. We are baptized in these things."

The Shadowlander made a threatening step around the table toward him, holding out the dagger, but Smirk remained unfazed.

"End this foolishness, Stranger," Smirk said. "You are no assassin, nor are you a warrior. This sort of game is quite beyond you."

"I'm sorry for this, I really am," the Stranger said, making to lunge for Smirk, but the Forsaken pirate captain was swifter, hurling his silver goblet at the Stranger, catching him on the forehead with a metallic clang and a splash of blackwine.

The Stranger cursed, bringing his free hand to his head, where blood flowed from the wound he'd received.

"Forsaken Southlander," the Stranger said. "You wounded me."

"The least I could do, under the circumstances, wouldn't you agree?" Smirk asked.

Not wanting to give the Shadowlander time to recover himself, Smirk drew a silver dagger from his scabbard, but the Stranger had already parted the Veil, the air shimmering behind him, as he dove through it, evading Captain Smirk.

Though he'd never faced one in combat, he knew the way of the Shadowlanders, and quickly turned up the wicks on his lanterns, bathing his cabin in light, to best banish the shadows. A capable Shadowlander would strike from those shadows, jabbing him with the poisoned dagger and being done with it.

"Best go back from whence you came, Stranger," Smirk said, going to where the shadows were faintest in his cabin, blade out, ready. He gazed at the silver goblet on the floor, and the spilled blackwine that was soaking into the rich carpet he'd bought many years before in Ankora.

Though he was prepared for it, the counterattack didn't come, even as agonizing moments passed in silence, with only his breathing keeping Smirk company.

Captain Smirk kept his lanterns burning bright throughout the night, but the Stranger had not returned, and the pirate prince did not sleep a wink on his way back to Vantiokh.

Ten

The slaughter outside of Fiss'Q's townhouse had been considerable, the blood pooling in the gutters. Nearly three dozen members of the Starslayers were piled up at her door, and the Deathmen had come there in force to remove them, with three carts arrayed side by side.

A dozen, black-robed acolytes heaved bodies onto the carts, taking their standard fee of whatever could be plucked from the bodies. As it stood, the Deathmen gained three dozen armored breastplates and shields, short swords, Arokhnai fighting spears, bows and arrows, and the signature helms of the Starslayers, which bore the telltale star-shaped opening around their faces. That so many of the arrows and spears were silver-tipped made it a happy day indeed for the Deathmen.

Fiss'Q stood before the mountain of the dead, cleaning her sword with a purple cloth.

"It was many who came to thy door in the night, Senator," the head Deathman said, his face barely visible beneath his cowl, only his nose and jaw showing. All Deathmen bore a golden pendant from which dangled a well-polished golden skull.

"Not nearly enough," Fiss'Q said, watching the sunrise, as An'alta and her other servants emerged, stepping carefully through the broken doorway, where a Deathman was prying out the fighting spears.

"We are glad you survived, Milady," An'alta said.

"Thank you, An'alta," Fiss'Q said. "I'm glad you were unharmed, as well."

"You saw to that, Milady," An'alta said. "What next?"

"Have the Smiler brought up," Fiss'Q said, watching the Deathmen go about their work with such cold efficiency for which they were renowned throughout Arokhnai.

"Blackhelms, Milady," An'alta said, nodding as the City Watch approached, before disappearing to recover Taltos Smile.

A half-dozen City Watchmen of Arokhnai came to Fiss'Q's street, bearing the symbol of their station, three white towers on black shields. They wore white cloaks, black helms, and carried blackwood hewing spears, which were twice the length of the Arokhnai fighting spears being yanked from Fiss'Q's damaged door.

"Senator," one of the Blackhelms said, a bearded man of middle age, his beard bearing twin stripes of white that ran down his chin.

"Captain Goren," Fiss'Q said. "Your men arrived a bit late to keep the peace, I'm afraid."

"I'm sorry, Senator," Goren said. "We heard reports of a confrontation, but had to wait until morning. You know how dangerous the streets of Arokhnai can be after dark."

"Of course," Fiss'Q said. The Blackhelms were not ones to bestir themselves after sunset, content to spend most of their time in their minaret towers, when they were not

taking bribes. She wondered if Goren was on the payroll of her adversaries.

"Is everything under control, then?" Goren asked, watching the Deathmen finish piling the bodies into their carts. Everything went in neat stacks, whether armor, weapons, or bodies.

"Entirely," Fiss'Q said, snapping her fingers, having another one of her servants come forward with a bag of gold ingots, which she weighed in her hand, to verify the requisite heft. "I hope this is sufficient for the City Watch's troubles."

Goren gestured for one of his men to take the bag. He held it, gave it a test shake, then nodded to Goren with a smile on his face.

"Anything to keep the peace, Senator," Goren said, snapping a finger as he and his fellow Blackhelms made their way off her street.

"One day, I shall do something about the Blackhelms," Fiss'Q said to herself, marking the men. They had key protectors in the Shadow Senate, from senior members who had been present when Arokhnai had only had three minaret towers, instead of the current seven. The Blackhelms were nearly as old as Arokhnai, and maintained a host of proud and pointless traditions. *One day,* Fiss'Q told herself. *When I am Shadow Lord, I will do something about them.*

"Mistress," An'alta said, distracting Fiss'Q from her reverie. "The Smiler is gone."

"What?" Fiss'Q asked. "How?"

"He somehow slipped his bonds and escaped the secret room," An'alta said, looking particularly upset, nervously knotting her fingers. Fiss'Q ran into her townhouse, into

the welcoming shadow, and parted the Veil yet again, in hopes that she might see Taltos fleeing.

She could see his spirit flaring as he ran, heading down the alley behind Fiss'Q's home. Fiss'Q pursued him at once, knowing in the growing daylight, that her abilities would be increasingly limited, her opportunities to access the Shadowlands fewer. Even in the brightest day, shadows could be found. But they were more like pools of shadow, versus the sea of it at dawn and dusk, and in the comforting night.

Fiss'Q got ahead of Taltos and parted the Veil again, emerging in front of him.

"Taltos," Fiss'Q said, seeing the Smiler pivot without hesitating, heading down another alley, and vaulting swiftly up the narrow walls of the side streets as nimble as a jungle cat, until he reached the rooftops.

She did not wish to waste time pursuing the Smiler, but felt the desire to say something to him, after all. He was heading for the Courtyard of Consequences.

Fiss'Q reentered the shadows, emerging again just ahead of Taltos, throwing out the flat of her blade to catch him across the knees. Her sword struck him as intended, and Taltos grunted at the impact, tumbling flawlessly onto the roof tiles.

"Taltos, stop running," Fiss'Q said. "I'm not going to recapture or harm you."

Taltos paused, turning. He had pulled his tunic over his face as if it were a shroud.

"The mercenary, Kyree, gave up his employer," Fiss'Q said. "You don't need to keep running. I have my answer. And I need answers from you. What do you know of Clan Smirk?"

The Southlander's pink eyes were the only thing she could see, beyond a thatch of snow-white hair sticking out from his black shroud.

"As much as anyone," Taltos said. "Pirates and smugglers. They smuggled my sisters and me into Arokhnai."

"At the behest of whom?" Fiss'Q asked.

"Our client," Taltos said.

"Tell me who your client is," Fiss'Q said. "Please."

"I cannot. I am recovering Trinna and Torina from your grisly and blasphemous display," Taltos said.

"Go ahead," Fiss'Q said. "But not now. Under the cover of night would be better. The Blackhelms will be after you, I can assure you, if you attempt it now."

"I have failed in the execution of my contract," Taltos said.

"What if I offered you a new contract?" Fiss'Q said. "You said yourself, Trinna negotiated it on your behalf, didn't she? So, for you, there is no shame. It was her contract, not yours. You were merely subcontracted by her."

The Southlander paused and reflected on this. "And you're going to do what, exactly? Buy out your own contract as part of your negotiation with me?"

"Yes," Fiss'Q said. "That, or I'm going to kill you here and now. What I'm giving you is a chance, if you would only see, you stubborn boy."

Taltos considered this, for Southlanders lived and breathed contracts. It was a language they understood completely.

"So, permit me to renegotiate a contract with you," Fiss'Q said. "You take your sister and cousin and leave Arokhnai. You head back to Vantiokh, if that's what you want. Or you head somewhere else. For this, I pay you the balance of the contract taken out on me, and half again. Tell me who your sister's client was, and I'll do this for you."

"Why would you do this?" Taltos asked. "We tried to kill you."

"You're young," Fiss'Q said. "Inexperienced. I don't want to kill you. Your sister and cousin forced my hand. But I've had time to consider you. You didn't dishonor yourself; you were simply being used by others. They were trying to create an inciting incident that would bring war between our cities. You were a pawn in someone else's game. I can hardly fault you for that."

"I have a counter offer," Taltos said. "You return our masks to us, as well as our weapons, and the bodies of my kin, and I will consent to your terms for the agreed-upon sum."

It was a curious moment, the two of them—Shadowlander and Southlander on the tiled rooftops of Arokhnai, negotiating terms, in the growing light of the day, as the shadows of the minaret towers shortened, and the Great Clock Tower tolled.

"I will honor those terms," Fiss'Q said. She could see the Smiler was still uncertain whether she could be trusted. And, for her part, Fiss'Q was not sure if she could trust Taltos, either.

"Why the change of heart, Shadowlander?" Taltos asked. "Assuming you even have a heart."

Fiss'Q pondered how to answer without further wounding the already badly scarred pride of the Smiler.

"As I said, you and your sisters were being used," Fiss'Q said. "Someone is trying to throw Arokhnai into war with Vantiokh. And I don't want that to happen. Our cities would both be greatly harmed by war. And, I think that

might be part of someone's still larger agenda. I need to investigate that. I could use allies in that endeavor."

Taltos scoffed behind his shroud.

"You think very highly of yourself, to think that your life could have launched a war with Vantiokh," Taltos said.

"I'm a Senator of Arokhnai," Fiss'Q said. "That matters."

"I'm sure it does," Taltos said. "In your Republic, at least."

Fiss'Q felt exposed atop the roof, with the minaret towers looming in the distance. In her mind, it was only a matter of time before a Blackhelm glanced over and saw them, and she made it a policy not to pay the City Watchmen more than one gratuity a day.

"Proud and ancient Arokhnai does not suffer insults lightly," Fiss'Q said. "Now, come with me beyond the Veil. We shall go back to my home and complete our contract."

"Swear to me this is not some ruse," Taltos said.

"I swear to you," Fiss'Q said. "I will honor our agreement fully. You swear to me that you will not attempt to kill, disable, or otherwise bring me harm."

"I swear it," Taltos said.

Fiss'Q parted the Veil, and held out her hand, which the Smiler reluctantly took. The two of them entered the Veil together, and vanished in the shadows as the morning sun began to bake the green roofing tiles of Arokhnai, before any Blackhelms were the wiser for it.

✣ ✣ ✣

Eleven

Taltos was wonderstruck upon returning to the here and now, in Fiss'Q's home. She wasted no time taking her shadowbox off the wall, carefully removing the smiling masks, which she handed over to Taltos. He replaced his own mask, the ghastly white smile of the thing bringing him a visible measure of comfort, while An'alta and the others blanched, uncertain of their mistress's plan, terrified of the deadly little Smiler standing free among them.

"Draw up papers, An'alta," Fiss'Q said, slipping a note to her servant, which reflected the numbers she'd negotiated with Taltos beyond the Veil.

"It is a beautiful place, your Shadowland," Taltos said. "Forlornly endless, and yet, enchanting. I can see why it might entice you."

"The Shadowlands are everywhere," Fiss'Q said. "They run through everything. Each night, the Prince of Shadows reigns, only to see His domain recede over the course of every day. But within the Shadowlands, He rules in perpetual twilight."

"I'm surprised you don't stay there," Taltos said. "It is a more beautiful place than even your lovely and ancient

Republic of Arokhnai. A sea of obsidian and onyx, radiant to behold."

"One day," Fiss'Q said. "One day, I'll part the Veil and never deign to return to the here and now. But not today."

An'alta, tidy, sure-handed little scribe that she was, held out the stylus for Fiss'Q to take. The Senator admired the young girl's penmanship. Good penmanship was a harbinger of one's skill with a sword. If An'alta's penmanship held, then she would, one day, become a very mighty swordswoman. Fiss'Q would make sure of this. Fiss'Q patted her head, and An'alta smiled back at her uncertainly.

Fiss'Q signed the contract, and held the stylus out to Taltos, who carefully reviewed the document, reading every line. When it was to his satisfaction, he signed it as well.

"Let there be no bad blood between your mighty clan and me," Fiss'Q said. "I have treated with you fairly. But I should warn you that my enemies will still be keen to bring you down, should they find you."

"They will not find me," Taltos said. Fiss'Q handed the slip to An'alta, instructed her to fetch some of her stronger-armed manservants to get the appropriate amount of gold from her personal vault.

"With the amount I am paying you, you should be able to impress your Grandmaster as to your merit," Fiss'Q said.

"Yes," Taltos said. "He is just as likely to send me right back to Arokhnai, with two new compatriots, and a new mission of his choosing."

"Should that happen, I hope we will meet as friends and allies," Fiss'Q said.

"We shall see," Taltos said.

"When night falls," Fiss'Q said. "We shall head to the Courtyard of Consequences, to recover your kin. It will

be unguarded, as is our custom. Once you recover them, you should flee to whatever safe house you and your kin arranged, and make good your escape from Arokhnai. I leave that to you, but warn you that the harbor will be well-guarded, and the conspirators who sought to use me in their bid for war with Vantiokh will bring you to considerable harm, should they find you."

"Your adversaries won't find me," Taltos said.

"They are Shadowlanders, like me," Fiss'Q said. "They can find you, if they go looking."

"Not like you," Taltos said. "They are not like you at all, I think."

"At any rate," Fiss'Q said. "Be very careful and flee Arokhnai. Warn your Grandmaster about the plot I believe I have uncovered. Tell him to be wary of petitioners in this city. Warn him of Clan Smirk's ambitions."

"He will be quite cross with me for freelancing," Taltos said.

"No," Fiss'Q said. "It was only your sister who inked that deal. You were simply a loyal brother. Make sure he understands that. You return as a loyal son of Vantiokh."

Fiss'Q handed Taltos the shadow box with the remaining masks, which he took with a nod. "We'll make for the Courtyard at dusk, when the shadows are long on the streets of Arokhnai."

Twelve

They reached the Courtyard as planned, Taltos having adopted a disguise as a Deathman. Of course, the Deathmen had no stake in the business of the Courtyard, but it would prove a useful disguise once he was gone from that place.

While he took down his sister and cousin, Fiss'Q parted the Veil and scanned the Courtyard, looking for signs of life. Of course, there were all manner of souls in their little homes, tending to business in their way, otherwise heedless of what was going on.

What Fiss'Q was looking for was someone who was out of place, paying attention to what they were doing, intently eyeing the opportunity for attack.

In that moment, there was no one in that position, and Fiss'Q dared to part the Veil again and return to Arokhnai proper, where Taltos had bundled his kin on the cart.

"This is goodbye, then, Senator," Taltos said, holding out his hand, which Fiss'Q shook. "Thank you for this small solace, however belatedly attained."

"You're welcome," Fiss'Q said. "Remember me favorably when you treat with your Grandmaster."

"You will never be forgotten," Taltos said, and spurred the horse onward, clattering free of the Courtyard, looking like nothing so much as a Deathman, as he vanished into the onrushing night.

Fiss'Q parted the Veil yet again, to take yet another look, when a silver bolt struck her in her shoulder, from the Veil to the here and now, knocking her off her feet.

She cursed, feeling the burn of the silver in her shoulder, as she saw the Shadowlander step out of the Veil, regarding her with caustic caution. It was Jhosia, who bore a breech-loading Arokhnai crossbow, loading it with another silver-tipped bolt. He glowered at her, a nasty cut at his forehead, only recently bandaged.

"Your sentimentality will be your undoing, Fiss'Q," Jhosia said. "Or your theatricality. I can't be sure which, at the moment."

Fiss'Q cursed, wounded as she was by the silver bolt. Jhosia locked the crossbow with a snap of his wrist, the string pulled taut by the well-oiled lever mechanism.

"You look like you've seen some action, yourself, Jhosia," Fiss'Q said.

"I have," Jhosia said. "Ah, precious silver, to keep us tethered to the here and now. If only the mundanes knew how easy—if costly—it is to contain us. Can't have you flitting about, now can we?"

Fiss'Q drew her sword, while Jhosia looked on with amusement, keeping himself at a safe distance.

"You know, I didn't expect you to show mercy," Jhosia said. "It was the one true failure of my plan. I expected you to snuff out those assassins like candles in the Hall of Shadows. And when you put them on display here, I thought that would be the perfect inciting incident."

Fiss'Q tried to pull the bolt from her shoulder, but Jhosia raised the crossbow.

"Don't remove it," Jhosia said. "If you do, I'll simply shoot you again. As many as it takes, Fiss'Q."

The two of them wheeled through the octagonal Courtyard of Consequences, the wounded warrior woman and the crossbow-wielding conspirator.

"We *need* a good war, Fiss'Q," Jhosia said. "After Arokhnai ended slavery, we had to do something, don't you agree? The other Slaver Cities will think we've gone soft. And Vantiokh has always coveted our position, perhaps even more than Uriokh, Ansible, or the others. They're the perfect target."

Jhosia was beaming, stalking after Fiss'Q at a distance, like a hunter, while she kept trying to approach him, the cursed silver-tipped bolt throbbing in her shoulder.

"War will be just what we need," Jhosia said. "Vantiokh will be our window to the Northlands, once we exterminate Clan Smile and enslave the other Forsaken. The Southlanders need to be slaves again, don't you think? They served the Sorians so very well. They'll serve us, too. And you can go to your death knowing that you made it all happen. I wanted you to know that, Fiss'Q."

"I don't see how," Fiss'Q said.

"It's simple, really," Jhosia said, as a company of Starslayers entered the Courtyard from all corners, cutting off her escape. "Your gallant challenge notwithstanding, what happened was the Smiler in your custody escaped, and you were killed attempting to apprehend him. And I, eager to avenge your death. I will pass a resolution in the House of Shadows declaring war on Vantiokh for their part in assassinating one of our own. We'll have someone

from the Guild of Sculptors make an obsidian statue in your honor, Fiss'Q. You'll be ensconced in the Hall, memorialized. I'll light a candle for you, myself."

The Starslayers lowered their fighting spears, cutting off any escape, and Fiss'Q hefted her greatsword, preparing for the end.

"Commander Kyree?" Fiss'Q called out.

"Here, Senator," Kyree said.

"As we agreed," Fiss'Q said, prompting Jhosia to whip his head around in shock.

"Yes," Kyree said. "Double whatever Jhosia paid us."

"Precisely so," Fiss'Q said.

"What?" Jhosia said. "Nonsense. Kyree, we had an agreement."

"I came to other, more agreeable terms with Senator Fiss'Q," Kyree said.

"Bloody mercenary. I'll triple what she's paying you," Jhosia said.

Then the Veil parted, and Q'rr'k emerged, carrying his curved sword, with Alburelle at his side.

"I thought you might say that," Fiss'Q said. "So, I had already informed Q'rr'k of my situation."

Jhosia, upon seeing the Shadow Lord standing there, and Alburelle at his side, would've blanched if he were able to.

"Senator Jhosia," Q'rr'k said. "You're charged with conspiracy to commit treason, as well as the attempted assassination of a fellow member of the House of Shadows. Lay down your weapon."

Jhosia, the eloquent, cursed Fiss'Q out. "You took a bolt from me *deliberately?*"

"Yes," Fiss'Q said. "I had to do something to keep you here. I counted on you to want to gloat a little, before you finished me."

Jhosia fired the crossbow at Fiss'Q, who deflected the incoming bolt with a timely turn of her blade, the bolt shattering at it struck her adamantine sword, sending sparkling shards of silver and splinters of blackwood everywhere.

Then he parted the Veil, only to have a silver net thrown down upon him from some other Shadowlanders in the service of Q'rr'k—Hadra Blackspear and Ky'la Sharp—two other, younger protégés of Q'rr'k's. They were both as tall and lean as Fiss'Q was. The net descended upon Jhosia, holding him fast to the here and now.

"No, Jhosia," Q'rr'k said. "You don't get to run. Not from us, not from this, and not from me. Hang him from the beam. Starslayers, stand watch and know that your lives are forfeit if Jhosia isn't here in the morning. Jhosia, you're going to face your punishment tomorrow for the crime of treason. That punishment is death."

"I made no such plan," Jhosia said.

"No, it was Captain Tobias Smirk," Kyree said. "He treated on your behalf with my own Captain Arven."

"You have no proof of this," Jhosia said.

"I have proof of it," Fiss'Q said. "The Smilers you contracted to assassinate me were smuggled into Arokhnai by Smirk. I believe his ship is the *Arcana*, yes?"

Jhosia glared at her through the silver netting.

"It is," Kyree said. "And we have the contract in our possession."

Fiss'Q watched the Starslayers hang Jhosia up where the Smilers had been hanging before. He looked like a prize fish, caught in that silver net, gape-mouthed and terrified. For a Shadowlander, who could live forever, there could be no greater price to pay than this.

"Q'rr'k's pet to the end," Jhosia said, his lips curled in a fanged snarl. "And you, Alburelle. I'll pay you back for your treachery as well."

Alburelle shook her head. "No, Jhosia, I'm afraid you will not. We're already liquidating your assets. You'll go before the Prince of Shadows tomorrow as a pauper."

Fiss'Q pried the silver bolt from her shoulder with a pained grunt, dropping it to the cobblestones of the courtyard. She gave her arm a test swing, wincing at the pain, but confident in her ability to recover from it. It would be the Silver Sword for Jhosia. He would face execution in the Courtyard of Consequences, before the entirety of the Shadow Senate, with Fiss'Q as the one swinging the blade.

"He won't be going anywhere, Alburelle," Fiss'Q said. "Not when he's killed by the Silver Sword. He'll remain here. No Shadowlands for you, Jhosia. Your headless shade will walk Arokhnai for eternity, as a silent warning to others."

"I'll haunt you, Fiss'Q," Jhosia said, recovering his tongue. "Until the end of your days, I will haunt your steps."

"I can live with that," Fiss'Q said. "But you, I'm afraid, cannot. The Silver Sword will ensure that tomorrow will be your last day on Irth."

"Are you up to the task, Fiss'Q?" Q'rr'k asked, eyeing her wounded shoulder with a degree of irony that only he could conjure up so readily.

"I'll be ready, Q'rr'k, have no fear," Fiss'Q said, giving Jhosia a smile. "I'll try to make it a clean cut, but no promises."

"You owe me, you know," Q'rr'k said. "Yet again."

"I know," Fiss'Q said. "But I should think saving Arokhnai from an unnecessary war would count for something."

"We shall see," Q'rr'k said. "I'm going to see if I can find this *Arcana*, and her captain."

"You should leave Captain Smirk to me," Fiss'Q said, although she hardly felt up to the task of hunting down a Forsaken pirate captain.

"Another time, my darling," Q'rr'k said, winking at her, before parting the Veil with Alburelle, leaving Fiss'Q wounded and alone in the Courtyard of Consequences. She only had a traitor and a number of rapacious mercenaries, and her nameless greatsword for company. Hadra and Ky'la, her sister-rivals, looked on with amusement. Hadra, wrapped in a goldenrod tunic, with her adamantine hewing spear in hand, and Ky'la dressed in a sea green, octagon-patterned wrap, with her rapier and stiletto at her narrow hips. They both looked like they dearly wanted someone to start something.

"Don't worry, Fiss'Q," Hadra said. "We'll make sure he stays put for his date with the Silver Sword."

"Yes," Ky'la said. "Go home, tend to your wounds, Senator. We'll guard Longshadow."

Fiss'Q looked at them both, who reminded her of younger versions of herself, and smiled at them, and to herself, her fangs caressing her lips. As the moon rose over the horizon, bathing the courtyard in moonlit shadows, it promised to be a lovely evening, and a still more glorious tomorrow.

FINIS

A Note on the Type

The text of this book is set in Adobe Jenson Pro, an old-style serif typeface drawn for Adobe Systems by its chief type designer Robert Slimbach. Its Roman styles are based on a text face cut by Nicolas Jenson in Venice around 1470, and its italics are based on those created by Ludovico Vicentino degli Arrighi fifty years later.

Nicholas Jenson (1420–1480) was a French engraver, pioneer, printer and type designer who carried out most of his work in Venice, Italy. Jenson acted as Master of the French Royal Mint at Tours, and is credited with being the creator of one of the finest early Roman type faces. Nicholas Jenson has been something of an iconic figure among students of early printing since the nineteenth century when the aesthete William Morris praised the beauty and perfection of his roman font. Jenson is an important figure in the early history of printing and a pivotal force in the emergence of Venice as one of the first great centers of the printing press.

Ludovico Vicentino degli Arrighi (1475–1527) was a papal scribe and type designer in Renaissance Italy. He turned to printing in 1524 and designed his own italic typefaces for his work, which were widely emulated. His last printing was dated shortly before the sack of Rome (1527), during which he was probably killed.

Composed by Clever Crow Consulting and Design,
Pittsburgh, Pennsylvania

Acknowledgments

I would like to thank all of my readers, who offered their time, attention, and opinions to the writing and revision of this book. I would also like to thank Christine Marie Scott of Clever Crow Consulting and Design in Pittsburgh for her wonderful cover art and her invaluable assistance with the layout of these pages.

About the Author

Dane Vale lives in Chicago, where he conjures up Sword & Sorcery and Fantasy fiction when he's not relentlessly critiquing his twin brother's writing. He owns at least one spear, dodges drunk texts from Dionysus, and believes that there should be more megaliths in America. He cooks Italian food with verve, and has a bond with wolves and crows. His favorite cities are Knossos, Carthage, Constantinople, Venice, and Paris. **RealDaneVale.com**

NOSETOUCH PRESS

Nosetouch Press is an independent book publisher
tandemly based in Chicago and Pittsburgh.
We are dedicated to bringing some of today's most
energizing fiction to readers around the world.

Our commitment to classic book design in a digital
environment brings an innovative and authentic
approach to the traditions of literary excellence.

*We're Out There™

NOSETOUCHPRESS.COM

Science Fiction | Fantasy | Urban Fantasy | Horror
Folk Horror | Occult | Supernatural | Gothic | Weird

*Visit realdanevale.com
for interviews, maps, and more
from Sagas of Irth!*